BUZZ AROUND THE TRACK

They Said It

"Oh, yes, I definitely like looking into the cerulean-blue depths of Dr. Foster's eyes. What I don't like is her drawing attention to the scar that could destroy my career."
—Trey Sanford

"He caught me staring, but so what? He's my patient. I have every right to observe him. And, yeah, okay, he also kissed me, but it was just a friendly act of appreciation. I've had other patients kiss me. Not on the mouth, and not the way he did. Still, it didn't mean anything."
—Dr. Nicole Foster

"I don't know what's going on with Trey's driving. Whatever it is, it needs to be fixed, and soon."
—Adam Sanford

"I can't believe a famous racecar driver likes *my* sister. But does he care enough about her to share all of his secrets?"
—Dave Foster

KEN CASPER,

aka K. N. Casper, author of more than two dozen books for Harlequin, figures his writing career started back in the sixth grade when a teacher ordered him to write a "theme" explaining his misbehavior over the previous semester. To his teacher's chagrin, he enjoyed stringing just the right words together to justify his less-than-stellar performance. That's not to say he's been telling tall tales to get out of scrapes ever since, but...

Born and raised in New York City, Ken is now a transplanted Texan. He and Mary, his wife of thirty-five-plus years, own a horse farm in San Angelo. Along with their two dogs, six cats and eight horses—at last count!—they board and breed horses and Mary teaches English riding. She's a therapeutic riding instructor for the handicapped, as well.

Life is never dull. Their two granddaughters visit several times a year and feel right at home with the Casper menagerie. Grandpa and Mimi do everything they can to make sure their visits will be lifelong fond memories. After all, isn't that what grandparents are for?

You can keep up with Ken and his books on his Web site at www.kencasper.com.

RUNNING WIDE OPEN

Ken Casper

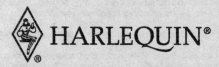

TORONTO • NEW YORK • LONDON
AMSTERDAM • PARIS • SYDNEY • HAMBURG
STOCKHOLM • ATHENS • TOKYO • MILAN • MADRID
PRAGUE • WARSAW • BUDAPEST • AUCKLAND

Recycling programs
for this product may
not exist in your area.

ISBN-13: 978-0-373-18527-6

RUNNING WIDE OPEN

Copyright © 2009 by Harlequin Books S.A.

Ken Casper is acknowledged as the author of this work.

NASCAR® and the NASCAR Library Collection® are registered
trademarks of the National Association for Stock Car Auto Racing, Inc.

To Marsha Zinberg and Stacy Boyd
Thanks for the privilege of letting me be part of the team

To Mary
The beginning, the middle and the end of every story
The adventure never ends

NASCAR HIDDEN LEGACIES

The Grossos

Dean Grosso
m.
Patsy Clark Grosso

Patsy's brother

— Kent Grosso
(fiancée Tanya Wells)

— Gina Grosso
(deceased)

— Sophia Grosso
(fiancé Justin Murphy)

Patsy's cousin

Kent's agent

The Clarks

Andrew Clark
(divorced)

Garrett Clark ⑯
(Andrew's stepson)

Jake McMasters ⑧

Kane Ledger ⑦

The Claytons

Dean's best friend

Steve Clayton ⑩

— Mattie Clayton ⑭

Business partner

Damon Tieri ⑪

The Cargills

Alan Cargill (widower)

Nathan Cargill ⑤

The Branches

Maeve Branch
(div. Hilton Branch) m.
Chuck Lawrence

— Will Branch ②

— Bart Branch

— Penny Branch m.
Craig Lockhart

— Sawyer Branch
(fiancée
Lucy Gunter)

① *Scandals and Secrets*
② *Black Flag, White Lies*
③ *Checkered Past*
④ *From the Outside*
⑤ *Over the Wall*
⑥ *No Holds Barred*
⑦ *One Track Mind*
⑧ *Within Striking Distance*
⑨ *Running Wide Open*
⑩ *A Taste for Speed*
⑪ *Force of Nature*
⑫ *Banking on Hope*
⑬ *The Comeback*
⑭ *Into the Corner*
⑮ *Raising the Stakes*
⑯ *Crossing the Line*

THE FAMILIES AND THE CONNECTIONS

The Sanfords

Bobby Sanford
(deceased)
m.
Kath Sanford

- Adam Sanford ①

- Brent Sanford ⑫

- Trey Sanford ⑨

The Hunts

Dan Hunt
m.
Linda (Willard) Hunt
(deceased)

- Ethan Hunt ⑥

- Jared Hunt ⑮

- Hope Hunt ⑫

- Grace Hunt Winters ⑯
(widow of Todd Winters)

The Mathesons

Brady Matheson
(widower)
(fiancée Julie-Anne Blake)

- Chad Matheson ③

- Zack Matheson ⑬

- Trent Matheson
(fiancée Kelly Greenwood)

The Daltons

Buddy Dalton
m.
Shirley Dalton

- Mallory Dalton ④

- Tara Dalton ①

- Emma-Lee Dalton

CHAPTER ONE

HIS TAIL WAS SLIDING out from under him, the rear tires skidding to the right, up the steep bank of Turn Two. He'd told his crew chief he was running loose. Ethan assured him they'd fixed the problem. A wedge in the suspension during the last pit stop, his second. Three pounds less air in the outside back tire.

Damn, his ass was going into a full swerve now, veering up the side of the asphalt hill.

Two cars screamed past him on the inside, below him. He sailed into a counterclockwise rotation, the wall behind him, above him. Trey steered to the right in an attempt to regain traction. Not soon enough. Jem Nordstrom smashed into him broadside. They plowed forward together down onto the straightaway.

Not for long. Suddenly Trey was rolling sideways.

Over and over and over.

The tube-steel cage of Car No. 483, the snug fit of the custom seat and the five-point harness kept him from being tossed around like the proverbial rag doll, but the bounces still weren't gentle. He instinctively brought his right hand up across his chest toward his left shoulder.

Bang! Bang! Bang!

The direction changed and Trey found himself flipping like a gymnast across an Olympic pad. One more rotation, this time in slow motion, then all movement ceased.

He was light-headed; no, he was upside down. Light-headed, too. Assess and act. He took a deep breath, reached once more across his chest, started to release his harness and realized his left arm wasn't cooperating.

Broken? No pain. Not yet, at least.

He had to get out of the car. Hanging upside down wasn't good.

He struggled with his right hand to release the clasp, then squirmed his way out of the window opening. The pavement beneath him was hot and sticky. The acrid stench of asphalt and burned rubber scorched his nostrils.

A twist of his head to the right brought a cockeyed view of vehicles approaching. Trucks.

He'd pulled his legs nearly free of the car by the time the first vehicle stopped close by and made it to a three-legged-dog position when strong hands gripped his elbows.

"My shoulder!" He forced the words out between his teeth. "The left."

The man holding it relaxed his upward pressure but continued more gently to support the arm.

Trey wasn't sure exactly when the stretcher materialized. He eased himself onto it and closed his eyes.

He closed his eyes, feeling guilty about leaving other people in charge of what was happening to him.

"Is my arm broken?" he asked as the gurney was being pushed into the boxlike ambulance.

"We'll know in a minute. Try to relax."

A joker. Relax. Ha! If his arm was broken he'd be out for the rest of the season. There was too much at stake. He lifted his right wrist to his chest, then slipped it back to his side.

He heard a vehicle door slam, felt dizzying motion and realized they were rolling again. To where? The infield care center, of course.

A guy was by his side, wrapping a blood-pressure cuff on Trey's right wrist, an earnest expression on his face.

"My name is Jody. Tell me your name and what injuries you're aware of." He shined a penlight into Trey's right eye, then his left.

"I'm Trey Sanford. My left shoulder hurts."

Jody encased Trey's left hand in his as if they were shaking hands. "Can you squeeze?"

Trey winced in the process.

"Probably not broken," Jody murmured. "Could just be badly bruised. Maybe dislocated. We'll know for sure in a minute." He carefully strapped the arm to the side of the gurney.

Trey's mental processes were beginning to clear. DNF. Did Not Finish. Damn. He'd launched the season by winning the opening race at Daytona, but that had been a demonstration competition and didn't count for points. Since then his performance—and his team's—had been like a roller coaster. Still he'd been in the top ten going into this race at Charlotte. Now another DNF, his third. Even with his recent win in Talledega, making the Chase for the NASCAR Sprint Cup would be tough. So what? Sanfords didn't quit. At least, some Sanfords didn't.

The doors flew open and he was moving again, feetfirst.

"One thirty-five over ninety-two," he heard Jody report. "Pulse seventy-one. Conscious and alert. Pain in the left shoulder. Possible dislocation."

Trey wanted to object. The pain wasn't severe, just annoying. Nothing he couldn't handle.

"Curtain four," a female voice stated.

A very nice female voice. Confident and businesslike but not strident. Pleasant.

Trey rotated his head to the right. She was pretty, red-headed, wearing a white coat, a frown of concern on her pretty face. Blue eyes. Compassionate blue eyes. A man could—

She leaned over him. "I'm Dr. Foster. Tell me where you're hurting and what it feels like."

"Left shoulder," he said. They really were the most extraordinary blue eyes. "Dull ache now."

"Can you sit up for me?"

And beg? he nearly blurted out. "Sure."

The medic—what was his name? Jody—guided his legs as he swung them over the side of the gurney and then helped lever him into a sitting position. The room spun. Trey raised his right hand to his chest, dropped it.

"Let's open your uniform so I can take a look," ordered Dr. Foster, she of the enchanting blue eyes. *But, Doc, we've just met.*

Fighting giddiness, Trey used his right hand to unzip it down to the waist.

"Can you slip it off your right shoulder without hurting yourself?" The question made him feel like a little kid. *Now don't hurt yourself.* "If not, we can cut it," she added.

"I can do it."

With Jody's help, he managed to shrug the fitted garment off his right shoulder. Accepting a little more assistance, he extracted his arm and hand from the sleeve. The doctor and Jody then eased the left sleeve off the other shoulder.

The T-shirt underneath, soaked with perspiration, clung to his skin. He shivered in the air-conditioning.

"Cut the shirt off," she directed.

One-handed, Trey loosened the soggy cotton from his waistband in front, while Jody tugged it out in back. The scissors slithered like an icicle up his spine. After slicing the front, as well, the medic removed the two halves.

Visually assessing Trey's upper arm, Dr. Foster checked

his wrist pulse to ensure circulation in the damaged limb. She placed her hands on his left shoulder, moved the arm slightly while palpating the joint. Trey sucked in a breath involuntarily. She gently positioned his hand in his lap.

"Let's get an X-ray," she told Jody.

Minutes later, she was peering at an image on a nearby computer flat screen.

"As I suspected, your shoulder has been dislocated," she informed Trey. "I can reset it, but it'll hurt. Do you want something for pain?"

"Just do it, Doc."

"Help him onto his back," she instructed Jody. "Stabilize his chest and shoulders."

Her assistant had hardly moved into place, one hand resting on Trey's right shoulder, the other positioned under his right elbow, when the good doctor rotated Trey's left arm and gave it a sharp tug.

The action was so quick he didn't have time to brace himself, to tighten his muscles, which, he decided after it was over, was precisely what she'd wanted. The momentary high-voltage jolt was so unexpected, a startled groan barely had time to escape. Instantly the pain subsided to a dull, low-grade gnaw.

She instructed him to move his arm and shoulder slowly in certain directions.

He raised his open hand, clenched his fingers, tentatively at first, then with increasing confidence, rotated his arm, flinching only slightly at a residual twinge of soreness.

She took hold of his triceps and forearm above the wrist and folded the arm across his belly and studied his chest more closely. Her perceptive eyes roaming over his bare skin suddenly felt intimate, making him aware of her as a woman rather than a doctor. Uncomfortably aware.

"That scar." She pointed to a nearly four-inch-long, pencil-thin line that ran vertically above his left pectoral muscle. "Do you have a pacemaker, Mr. Sanford?"

Her eyes made contact with his. Oh, yes, he definitely liked looking into those cerulean-blue depths. What he didn't like was her drawing attention to the blemish that made him different.

"There's nothing wrong with my heart, Doc," he murmured in a warning undertone and hoped she got the message. "Trust me on that."

"But—" A question formed on her lips. Nice lips, too, he observed. She was about to ask it when a voice outside the curtain distracted them.

"I'm looking for Trey Sanford."

"I'm in here, Gaby," Trey called out.

The white drape was yanked aside and Gaby Colson stuck her head in. Almost immediately the rest of her five-foot-four frame followed. "You okay?"

"I am now, thanks to Dr. Foster here. She made sure all my body parts were in the right place."

Trey introduced the two women.

"So what happened?"

"Dislocated my left shoulder," he explained. "The doc here set it back where it belongs with one gentle tug."

"I'm an orthopedist. That's what I do." She removed the stethoscope from around her neck and stuffed it into her coat's right patch pocket. "Besides, I'm not sure you thought it was so gentle at the time." Her taunting smile was like an electrical charge, jolting him, producing heat.

"Ah, come on, Doc." He offered her his best grin. "It was just a little whimper."

She chuckled.

"Let's get you decent," Gaby said to Trey, "so you can go out there, make a clever remark or two about it being one hell of a ride today, then vamoose. I'll take over from there."

"We need to immobilize your arm," Dr. Foster reminded Trey.

"That won't be necessary," he objected.

"I tell you what, Mr. Sanford. You let me make the medical decisions, and I'll let you drive the cars."

Gaby snickered. "Ouch!"

"You're really cute when you're giving orders," Trey said.

Gaby rolled her eyes.

"I think those grease smudges on your face are adorable, too. Nice touch. Jody," Dr. Foster called out, "we'll use the six-inch."

The medic appeared with a large role of flesh-colored flex bandage, and the two of them commenced binding Trey's left arm across his chest.

"You dislocated your shoulder," she explained in a professional tone. "Keep it bound for at least three days. After that you can use a simple sling. If you don't, you'll be susceptible to dislocating it again, and every time you do it'll be easier to pop it the next time. You don't want that to happen."

"No, ma'am," he said the way he would answer his schoolteacher.

"Will he be able to drive next week?" Gaby asked.

"If he follows medical advice. I recommend he get the shoulder examined by his regular physician in a couple of days to ensure he's mending properly." She again visually examined his torso and shoulders. "If you normally do weight training, lay off for a couple of weeks. Then you can resume gradually."

Seemingly satisfied with the job she'd done, Dr. Foster told him he could get dressed. She went back to the computer in the corner of the cubicle and started tapping on the keyboard.

Jody and Gaby helped Trey pull his tacky uniform back up, his left arm inside, his hand sticking out, as if it were pointing to his right shoulder.

"Thanks, Doc," Trey called out as he jumped off the thin mat. "You've got one hell of a bedside manner."

She spun around on her low stool. "It's a gurney, not a bed."

"Well, maybe next time we can do a bed." He watched her almost blush, but then she shook her head.

"You'll be sore for a few days and tender for perhaps a week, but you should fully recover if you don't try to push it too fast, avoid violent motions and heavy lifting." Her eyes wandered to the spot under the uniform where she'd seen the scar. "About that scar—"

"Doc..." He leaned forward and placed his free arm around her, gave her a hug and whispered in her ear, "Shut up about the scar." He started to release her then, on an irresistible impulse, kissed her firmly on the lips. He wasn't sure whether it was the message or the kiss that made her stiffen, but it didn't matter. He liked the effect and the sense of power it gave him. "Thanks for your help," he added more loudly, aware that several people were watching.

"Give them a quick 'I'm fine' outside," Gaby reminded him impatiently, "and leave the rest to me."

As he approached the door, someone opened it, letting in the sounds Trey loved—the roar of unmuffled 850-horsepower engines screaming around the track in front of equally loud, excited fans. He could feel the ground beneath him tremble as the lead pack circled Turn Three.

He looked over his right shoulder. One kiss wasn't enough. She was watching, her expression now one of professional detachment—until their eyes met. Maybe not so detached after all. He turned again toward the door. They were waiting for him out there—the reporters with microphones, the cameramen with long lenses ready to zero in. For a moment he braced himself psychologically, brushed his right wrist across his chest. Trey stepped aggressively toward the open door, stopped and glanced back one more time. She hadn't moved, but color had suffused her cheeks. Seconds that seemed timeless ticked by, before he spun around, marched through the gaping doorway and was instantly assailed by questions. One kiss was definitely not enough.

NICOLE WATCHED HIM GO. He'd caught her staring, but so what? He was her patient; she had every right to observe his movements, to make sure he was physically fit for the circumstances he was in. Except he'd also kissed her. Just a friendly act of appreciation, she told herself. She'd had other patients kiss her. Not on the mouth, though, and not the way he had. Still, it didn't mean anything. He was Trey Sanford, after all. He had a reputation. She should probably be insulted by his audacity in kissing her, but it was fun.

She'd met several NASCAR drivers over the years, spent her share of time in the infield and garage areas, but she hadn't met Trey Sanford even though her best friend, Becky, had dated him for several months. Every time the crowd got together, Nicole had to work. He was every bit as handsome in person as he was in photographs and in live interviews, and she had to admit the guy intrigued her beyond the purely medical.

She couldn't help thinking about his slight hesitation when she asked if he had a pacemaker. *Nothing wrong with my heart.* Cute comeback. As for his message just before he kissed her—it had silenced her but hadn't answered her question. The scar on his chest was obviously the result of a surgical incision, one he clearly wasn't eager to talk about, so what kind of medical procedure had he undergone? Becky had never mentioned it and Nicole couldn't recall ever reading anything about him being hospitalized. Why was he so secretive about it?

Then she saw him swipe his right wrist across his chest, across the very spot where the cut had been made. Nothing more than a nervous habit, or was he in physical discomfort and didn't want to tell her? Had she missed something?

As the door closed behind him, shutting out the wall of noise on the other side, somebody called out, "You have the magic touch, Doc." She waved it off with an exaggerated grimace of annoyance, secretly smiled to herself and went to the corner of the mini-emergency room, to the password-protected computer that held the medical files of drivers and their team members. Dr. Halsey had asked her to fill in for him this weekend because his daughter had been in a car accident. There had been barely enough time to obtain NASCAR's approval for her to substitute, so Nicole hadn't had a chance to study the records before the race. Then, right after the green flag waved, a member of one of the other teams had come in with a cut bad enough to require half a dozen stitches.

She entered her temporary password, perused the alphabetical list of files available, found Trey Sanford's name and clicked. To her surprise she had to enter her password again. She did so. The file opened with a caveat that the information it contained was highly sensitive privileged medical information that was not to be discussed with anyone without the express permission of the patient.

Well, of course, she thought. That was standard medical ethics. Why this additional reminder? Then she saw the specially flagged entry and understood.

CHAPTER TWO

IT WAS HALF PAST SIX and springtime, so it would be hours yet before complete darkness fell, though the sun had already dipped behind the forested mountaintops, casting the valley in dusky shadow. A rain shower had ended a few minutes earlier, leaving the air sweet and damp. Brevard's sidewalks glistened, every tree and shrub washed clean.

Trey emerged from the antiques store where he'd taken refuge from the downpour, his unplanned purchase neatly wrapped in brown paper and tucked inside a plastic bag. He ambled to his car half a block away. After the crew meetings on Monday mornings he was supposed to have that afternoon off and all of Tuesday, too. It rarely worked out that way, however. Today he'd had two guest appearances in Asheville and an interview that hadn't been over until after three o'clock, but the rest of the day was his. He loved everything to do with NASCAR, but this rare opportunity during the racing season to spend a few leisure hours on his own was an extra treat.

He'd been to Transylvania County and the mountain town of Brevard many times, enjoyed the area's famous waterfalls and lush forests, but this afternoon had been especially pleasant. The only thing missing was company—of the female variety. He had a reputation for playing the field, of having a new girl hanging on his sleeve wherever he went. Thanks to several blogs he was even credited over the past several months with having a girlfriend down in old Mexico. Untrue, but he did nothing to discourage the rumors.

Trey wished he could have invited the pretty doctor who had reset his arm Sunday to tag along. However, not many people could slip away from their jobs on the spur of the moment to drive off to a little town in the Smokies for the afternoon, a busy doctor least of all. But he couldn't forget his last glimpse of her as he stood in the doorway of the infield care center. Their eyes had locked, and in that little moment out of time hers had told him she'd enjoyed the kiss as much as he had.

He unlocked his two-seater sports car and was about to put down the top and climb behind the wheel to drive home to Lake Norman when he heard an unmistakable sound. Bluegrass.

Smiling, he left the car top up, tossed his purchase onto the passenger seat and strolled in the direction of the vibrant harmonic strains.

They were coming from a music store a few doors down. Inside he saw half a dozen people sitting on old-fashioned wooden folding chairs. Facing them, seated in a semicircle, were the musicians. Ten or twelve of them. Fiddlers, guitarists, banjo and mandolin players. Trey recognized the tune, a classic: "Sally Goodin'." It was hard not to toe-tap to the compelling rhythm.

A woman listener near the door looked up over her shoulder at his entrance, paused a moment, then her brown eyes sparkled in recognition. She nodded an invitation for him to take one of the empty places. The chair squeaked as he sat down. A few other spectators turned and appeared to recognize him, as well, but they, too, took his presence in stride and granted him his privacy.

He sat through several numbers, some vocal, others

instrumental. The heritage of Scots-Irish melody and close, almost eerie harmony, combined with the bittersweet mixture of the joy and melancholy of generations of hard-living mountain people sent chills down his spine.

The instrumentalists ranged in age from a teenager on a five-string banjo to a leather-faced fiddler who was at least seventy.

It wasn't until a woman playing the guitar called a break that people rose and approached Trey. A few politely asked for autographs.

The teenage banjo player, a lanky young man who towered by several inches over everybody in the room, including Trey, came up to him with outstretched hand. "My name's Dave. My sister is Nicole Foster, the doctor who took care of you at the race when—"

Dr. Foster. Nicole Foster. He hadn't heard her first name yesterday. Nicole Foster, his former girlfriend Becky's friend.

"Sure," Trey responded with an amused chuckle. "I remember her." The spunky redhead with the sure hands and gorgeous blue eyes. The woman he'd kissed full on the mouth. "She had me fixed up in no time."

"Good race yesterday," Dave said.

"Until the accident."

"Man, that was spectacular. They kept showing it on TV."

A middle-aged man in a plaid shirt and tan chino pants joined them. Dave introduced him as Ernie. He had a violin case tucked under his left arm and shook Trey's hand, then turned to the young man. "I'm ready to leave now, son, if you are."

Trey perked up. "You need a lift home?" he asked Dave. "I'll be glad to take you."

"Thanks for bringing me, Ernie," Dave said. "I'll go back with Trey."

"See you next week, then." The older man nodded a farewell to the visitor and left the shop.

"Let me grab my banjo." Dave dodged away and returned a moment later with his instrument case. He called out goodbyes to the players who were still there.

"Where'd you learn to play?" Trey asked as they strolled in the direction of his car.

"Took guitar lessons when I was a kid. Play the mandolin, too, but the banjo's my favorite. You play anything?"

"I wish. My mother made me take piano lessons, but no amount of practice can make up for a lack of talent. You either have it or you don't. I don't."

They arrived at Trey's car. Dave eyed the shiny dark green sports convertible and whistled. "Cool."

Trey wondered how his passenger would ever squeeze his long-legged frame into it. The seat could go back a little more, but hardly enough to accommodate a guy who was at least six-four. He clicked the door release as he walked around to the driver's side. "Hang on a minute while I put the top down." He thumbed a button, and the engine started and settled into a soft purr. Trey pressed a third button, and the canvas top folded itself into the trunk space.

"Climb in," he invited Dave, "if you can."

Dave laughed. "Piece of cake. Jenny's car is bigger than this on the outside, but there's not much more legroom inside, especially when she has the bench seat pulled all the way forward so she can reach the pedals. I've learned to adjust." He reached under the bucket seat for the release, moved it back as far as it would go and maneuvered his gangly frame into the available space. "Neat," he cooed with admiration, running his hands over the soft leather upholstery and polished hardwood dashboard. He closed the door and fastened his seat belt.

"How come you're hitching tonight?" Trey asked,

when he stopped for a traffic signal that, at this hour, was blinking red.

"I don't have a car. Usually my girlfriend, Jenny, picks me up and drops me off. She plays the hammer dulcimer at our Monday-night sessions, but her mother wasn't feeling well today, so Jenny stayed home to take care of her. Since Ernie drives by my house on his way to town, I call him when she can't make it."

"No car yet, huh?"

"I don't even have a driver's license," Dave complained.

That struck Trey as odd. He and all his friends had gotten their licenses as soon as they were eligible. "How old are you?"

"Seventeen. I graduated from high school a few weeks ago."

"Early? Aren't most kids eighteen when they graduate?"

"I was in an accelerated program."

Which confirmed Trey's impression the kid was smart. "Didn't you take driver's ed in school?"

"I wish." Dave let out a frustrated breath. "I have epilepsy. Don't worry, I'm not going to start frothing at the mouth," he said sarcastically, his broad shoulders raised defensively. "People have these stupid ideas about epilepsy, like…" He seemed to catch himself, paused and relaxed his posture. "Actually," he continued more calmly, "I haven't had a seizure in over two years, but my CFS still wouldn't sign the papers for me to get a waiver."

Epilepsy? That came as a surprise. It was a rare condition. Or maybe the surprise was that Dave acknowledged having it so freely. He'd like to talk to the kid about it more, but first he had another question. "CFS?"

Dave snickered. "My control freak sister."

Trey chuckled. For a moment he tried to picture Dr.

Nicole Foster in black leather with a whip in her hand, but the image didn't come through. Instead he remembered the feel of her warm, firm hand on his shoulder as she popped his misaligned joint back into place. She'd been strong, sure and efficient. Controlling? Well, yeah. She'd made it clear who was in charge of his medical treatment. And perceptive. She'd noticed the scar. Had she discovered why it was there yet?

"Is your sister a neurologist, as well as an orthopedist?"

"Just an orthopedist, like our dad."

An orthopedist whose brother had epilepsy, and who worked at the infield care center at a NASCAR track. "Your dad still practicing medicine? Do they work together?"

"Our folks died in a plane crash eight years ago. Nicole's my legal guardian, so she's in charge."

Ah, that explained the resentful tone. "Pretty strict, huh?"

Dave grunted. "She's always getting in my face about something."

Trey didn't laugh, but he wanted to. The idea of getting in *her* face, lips to lips, was very appealing. CFS. He'd have to remember that. "You have any other brothers or sisters?"

"There's just the two of us. Turn right at the next corner."

A cell phone chirped. Trey recognized the melody of the "Wreck of Old No. 9." Dave fished the instrument out of his jeans back pocket. "Hi. How's your mom? That's good. Okay. I'll be over in a few minutes. Yeah, you know I do. See you in a few. Bye."

Dave closed the instrument. "Would you mind dropping me off at Jenny's place? Her mom's feeling better, but she's sleeping now. That'll give Jenny and me a little bit of time together."

"No problem. Where is it?"

"Take the next left."

Trey followed directions as Dave squeezed his cell phone back into his pocket.

"You going to call your sister and let her know where you'll be? Won't she be worried if you don't come home?"

"She's not there. Monday and Tuesday nights she works at the clinic in Hendersonville. She won't be home for hours yet, maybe not until after midnight."

Disappointing. One of the reasons he was driving the kid home was to see her again. It would have been nice if their days off had coincided.

"How will you get home from Jenny's?"

"It's just a short walk. There's a path through the woods. I do it all the time."

At Dave's direction, Trey turned down a narrow country lane. Jenny's house was a story-and-a-half saltbox, modest in size, plain and unpretentious.

"Thanks for the lift, Trey, er, Mr. Sanford."

Trey laughed. "You had it right the first time. It was nice meeting you, Dave. Say hello to Jenny for me." He was about to add that he should also say hello to his sister for him, but the kid had already unwound his legs from under the dashboard, grabbed the banjo case he'd set on the floor between his knees and with natural agility was up on his feet. He slammed the car door. "Thanks again."

Trey watched him run up the driveway and dart around the side of the narrow house. Must be quite a girl, Trey thought enviously and experienced once more the disappointment of not getting to see the kid's big sister. They'd met for a few minutes in a purely professional setting. The kiss notwithstanding, he'd be foolish to imagine she saw him as anyone but a patient. He doubted she'd even given him a second thought after she left the infield care center.

Why should she? Except that he was Trey Sanford, NASCAR driver, of the notorious Sanfords, and he had kissed her. He laughed at his own vanity as he slipped the car into gear and tooled down the street.

Four twenty-seven Grover Lane was the address Dave first gave him. Trey recalled passing Grover Lane at the last intersection. Backtracking, he turned onto the broader country road where larger homes lined both sides of the tree-canopied street. Even if Dr. Nicole Foster wasn't home, he could see where she lived.

Number 427 was no modest saltbox, more like a mansion. A big white Victorian house with a wide wraparound porch. Multipaned windows with black shutters lined the bottom and second floors. Three dormers, the middle one double-size, projected from the slate roof. Six steps led up the wisteria-framed central entranceway. Maple, pecan, hickory and pine trees towered behind the house and bordered its sides.

Peering at the classic beauty of the place, Trey pictured the woman he'd met gently rocking in one of the chairs or the cushioned glider on the porch.

Feeling unexpectedly lonely, he eased up on the brake, transferred his foot to the gas pedal and quietly drove away.

CHAPTER THREE

MIDMORNING ON TUESDAY Nicole was examining the X-ray of the patient she'd just seen. The woman had degenerative arthritis in her hip and would eventually need a replacement to get permanent relief from the pain she was experiencing. In the meantime a few simple changes in lifestyle and over-the-counter analgesics would go a long way toward alleviating the worst of her discomfort.

"Uh, Doc, there's someone here, a walk-in," her receptionist announced from behind her. "Says you treated him once before but—"

Nicole blanked the screen and swiveled around on her stool to face the door. She almost did a double take.

"I don't have his name in the system," Emily continued.

Tall, straight, dressed in a black T-shirt and stonewashed jeans, Trey Sanford hovered behind her, a grin on his handsome face.

"Oh…um," Nicole muttered, surprised to see him there. "That's okay, Em. I have a few extra minutes."

The other woman hesitated a moment. It was obvious to Nicole that she didn't recognize him, and if he'd given his right name—why wouldn't he?—it didn't mean anything to her, either. Emily was new to the area and apparently not a NASCAR fan—yet. As Nicole pondered these thoughts and recalled the events of two days earlier, Trey continued to smile, stepping back and moving briefly out of sight as Emily retreated. He reappeared, entered the room, and she closed the door behind him.

"Hey, Doc," he said, almost boyishly, "I happened to be in the neighborhood and thought I'd stop by and thank you for what you did for me Sunday." He raised both arms. "See? All the body parts are working fine."

"I'll be the judge of that." She couldn't help returning his grin.

"Hey, if you want to check over your handiwork more closely, I don't mind. I've always enjoyed playing doctor. Except in this case I guess it'll be the patient. Or should we call it show-and-tell?"

He'd been mildly flirtatious Sunday when he was in pain. Now… Was this the true Trey coming out? Her friend Becky had told her a mischievous sense of humor was one of his most endearing qualities. She'd forgotten to mention what a hunk he was in a clinging T-shirt. There was no question he spent time pumping iron.

"Have you been experiencing any pain?"

"Only in my heart from missing you."

She tried not to be amused by him, but of course she was. Still, she had to verify he was all right, and that meant a hands-on physical evaluation.

With a head-shaking snicker, she motioned him to the middle of the room. "Let me see you rotate both your arms in a circle."

"Sure." He pinwheeled his arms in opposite directions two sweeps each, stopped and reversed them. "See, no problem."

"Remove your shirt," she ordered.

He gazed at her impishly. "Anything you say, Doc."

She watched as he pulled the T-shirt out of his waistband and tugged it over his head. She couldn't help being aware of the way the light cast the well-toned ridges and valleys of his belly and chest in subtle relief. Having a sense of humor was important, but why hadn't Becky mentioned he also had a killer body?

What was the matter with her, Nicole asked herself. This man was a patient; she was a professional. She'd better start acting like one. She scrutinized the scar above his left pectoral. From more than a few feet away it was nearly invisible. Whoever had sutured it had been superbly skilled. "Turn around, please."

He did. Without hesitation or question. Having his back to her didn't help matters. Not only did he not have any blemishes to distract her, but his broad shoulders loomed even wider from behind, as they tapered down to his narrow, sinewy waist.

Approaching to within touching distance, she reached up, placed a hand on each warm deltoid and asked him to go through a series of movements. She could find nothing wrong—except for the unprofessional effect the sensation of his muscles flexing and tightening, pulling and loosening beneath her fingers was having on her. She was an orthopedist, she reminded herself again. He was a case. A body to be evaluated. Medically evaluated. This sensual awareness was unlike her and more than a little disconcerting.

She did her best to keep her tone neutral, though her heart was in her mouth as she felt him flex and rotate his joints. "That was quite a crash you were involved in Sunday. I watched reruns of it on TV last night. Absolutely spectacular. Is there any chance you had a seizure out there?"

He pulled away from her, though a second before he'd seemed perfectly content to lean conspiratorially into her caress. A moment passed. When he turned around to face her, he had his thumbs looped nonchalantly into the belt loops of his well-fitted jeans, but the tautness of his chest muscles communicated a different message.

"You've obviously gotten around to reading my medical profile, Doc." His voice was low and calm, but it was also laced with an accusatory note of annoyance. "So you know I have a VNS to prevent that."

Yes, she knew. She'd done her research after reading his confidential file. She'd learned why he had a surgical scar on his chest and why he dragged his wrist, or more precisely the magnetic band on his wrist, over it from time to time.

Because he had a Vagus Nerve Stimulator implanted directly below the collarbone.

A VNS was like a pacemaker, except instead of sending electrical impulses to the heart, it sent short bursts of mild stimulation to the brain via the left vagus nerve. The result was a steady rhythm of electrical current to the brain instead of the erratic bursts that caused epileptic seizures.

"Since your brother has epilepsy," he added with cheerful casualness, "I expect you're very familiar with seizure disorders and their treatments."

She flinched. Her gorgeous blue eyes widened in shock. It might have been comical, if he didn't also sense confusion that bordered on offense.

"You—you know about Dave?" she stammered. "But… how?"

He couldn't hold back a smile. He hoped it didn't come across as smug, but her question about whether he'd had a seizure on the track had irritated him on several levels, reminding him he was different, that he was vulnerable, and implying that he would put other people in danger for his own gratification. He was overreacting, but years of having to hide a condition he hated, that other people feared, made him oversensitive.

He would have time to despise himself later. At the moment, there was something satisfying in catching her off guard. Apparently Dave's Control Freak Sister didn't know everything going on in her brother's life. Equally obvious was that Dave didn't feel compelled to tell her about their meeting. For all his flaws—Trey liked to think he wasn't a vain man—he didn't consider himself naive, either. People didn't ask him for his autograph because he was another guy on the street. Since Nicole had mentioned meeting him to her brother, Trey had expected Dave to mention meeting him to her. Did that oversight represent a chink in her CFS protective armor?

Whatever the case, it made her that much more intriguing. Two days ago he'd met a dedicated, highly competent doctor who also happened to be a very attractive woman. Today he was meeting a woman who intrigued him.

"Your brother and I ran into each other last evening in Brevard," he said. "I guess he forgot to tell you."

Apparently the same thought had been going through her mind, for she looked distracted, annoyed. "I guess he did," she mumbled. "You can get dressed now."

Trey retrieved his shirt from the back of the chair and slipped it over his head. Instead of turning away, she stood a few feet away and watched him. Evaluating his shoulder movements, no doubt, but he found it unnerving, nevertheless, and stimulating at the same time.

"What were you doing in Brevard last evening?" she asked as he tucked his shirt into the waistband.

"After I finished up my PR appointments in Asheville, I had a few hours to myself, so I spent them indulging my passion for old and rare books. I was getting into my car to drive home when I heard the jam session in the music store and stopped in to listen. Dave is really good on the banjo."

"Yes, he is," she replied pensively. "Old books?" He watched doubt blossom and wane on her face. "You collect old books?"

Apparently he wasn't fitting into her stereotype of a NASCAR driver. He could have told her there were other NASCAR drivers who collected books and were avid readers with extensive and well-used personal libraries.

"As a matter of fact," he added, "I found a first edition of *The Catcher in the Rye*. In excellent condition, too. Still had the dust cover on it."

"How did you become interested in books?" she asked.

He was tempted to give her a flip reply about even being able to read them but decided the question wasn't a put-down. She was genuinely interested. Unlike epilepsy, book collecting wasn't something he had to hide.

"When I was a kid my father had a big stack of old automotive manuals that had been accumulating for years. All of them out-of-date, of course, so he told me to burn them. I started paging through them and found them fascinating. Automotive science was more mechanical and less electronic than it is today. No fancy computers to diagnose and fix problems. You did it by trial and error, with greasy fingers and a keen ear. Still do to some extent, of course, but it was more primitive fifty or more years ago. Anyway, the old manuals with their line drawings and fuzzy photographs intrigued me, so instead of destroying them, I began looking for others. You want an owner's manual for a 1916 Oakland touring car or a 1928 Duesenberg Model J? I've got 'em."

She smiled, reminding him once again how much he liked the way her blue eyes sparkled when she did. "Along with a first edition of *The Catcher in the Rye*," she noted.

"Most of the books on my shelves are technical, the majority of them dealing with cars, but there are other subjects, too," he acknowledged. "Like *Lady Chatterley's Lover*."

He wished they were somewhere more private, his motor

home, for instance, sipping wine and nibbling on cheese. He wondered if she liked baked Brie on crispy French bread with a chilled chardonnay or perhaps a zesty zinfandel.

"How about you?" he asked. "You like to read?"

She chuckled, appearing genuinely amused by the question. Okay, so it was an old chestnut. *Read anything interesting lately?*

"It may shock you to learn I've never read an automotive manual. I'm not even sure I've seen one. I've read so many medical books that my taste in reading for pleasure runs more to fiction, mostly family sagas, historical romances and Westerns."

"Fictionwise I'm more inclined to mysteries and thrillers," he acknowledged.

Small talk. An opportunity for each of them to learn a little more about the other. He liked that. He was about to ask who her favorite authors were when she said, "Dave told you he has epilepsy. Did you tell him you have a seizure disorder, as well?"

CHAPTER FOUR

A FAIR QUESTION. When one person disclosed a medical condition, it wasn't uncommon for others to reveal theirs.

"No, I didn't," Trey informed her. "Except for members of my family, my crew chief and a minimal number of top NASCAR officials, nobody knows I've had seizures. I'm sure you saw the note in my file specifying that under no circumstances is it to be discussed with anyone, publicly or privately."

"I understand my ethical responsibilities regarding medical confidentiality," she observed with an edge of indignation in her tone.

Damn. The rapport they'd been developing had been destroyed by one word: *epilepsy*. Why the hell did she have to go there? But since she'd brought the subject up, they might as well get it over with once and for all.

"I hope you understand, as well, why this is a particularly sensitive subject for me," he said. "The smallest hint of it in public would start rumors and speculation that could ruin my career."

She tilted her head in acknowledgment of what he said, but it also conveyed the impression she was dismissing his comments as exaggeration.

"I'm serious," he insisted.

Her brows arched. "I know you are. Let me ask you,

have you ever considered simply going public and avoiding all the problems associated with secrecy?"

"No." He didn't reckon there was any way to be more emphatic. "I shouldn't have to tell you there's a stigma attached to epilepsy. If I were to go public or someone else were to disclose my condition, my racing career as a driver would be finished, ended." He hated to admit even to himself how vulnerable that left him. At the moment he couldn't help resenting her for making him feel that way. He was living the life he loved, a good life, a multimillion-dollar-career life, and it could all be destroyed with a few careless words.

She sat on the low stool but faced away from the blank screen of the laptop. "You're right about common prejudices and misconceptions surrounding epilepsy. They're based on age-old superstitions and plain modern-day ignorance. I don't imagine there are many people in our society who attribute seizures to demon possession or angelic inspiration as they once did, but there also aren't enough people who understand that it's a noncontagious medical condition that can be controlled, even if we don't yet have a cure for it."

He took the straight-backed chair across from her and crossed his legs. "You won't get any arguments from me on those points."

"It seems to me the best way to dispel a stereotype is by the example of the exception to the rule."

"And I suppose you think I'm that exception."

She regarded him seriously. "Aren't you? You have a seizure disorder, yet you're a very successful NASCAR driver."

There might be some question about the *very successful* after Sunday's DNF, but that wasn't the real issue.

"Nice try, sweetheart." The moment the sarcasm slipped out he knew it was a mistake, because her face tightened. Apologizing was an option, but he rejected it. He wasn't the one on the offensive. She was. She was also questioning a decision that was none of her business.

She softened her expression. "You could inspire a lot of people."

"I seem to have a fair number of fans," he replied, "so I must be inspiring someone."

"You know what I mean." She tempered her exasperation with an encouraging smile.

"Do you understand what I mean? Do you have any idea what going public with a seizure disorder would cost me?"

She stared at him, but this time he didn't get the impression she saw him. "You're right," she said after a moment of thought. "Forget I asked."

Ah, the old guilt-trip gambit. He studied her, making it clear her ploy wasn't going to work. "Nicole, what's this all about?" She had an agenda, he was sure of that. He'd never met a woman who didn't, which was one reason his associations with them never lasted. "What is it you really want from me?"

She paused a moment. "My brother's epilepsy is under control now, but it hasn't always been, and the threat of seizures limits some of his opportunities—"

"Like not being allowed to drive."

"You know about that?"

"He told me."

She huffed. "He seems to have told you quite a lot. He's usually very reticent about discussing his problems. Then again, as you say, you're an inspiration."

Trey knew if he waited long enough she'd get around to answering his question. The secret was not to get her off track with another one, so he let the silence linger.

"How about telling him you have a seizure disorder, too, so he'll know it doesn't have to rule his life?"

"He doesn't need to know my medical condition to

understand that. Your brother strikes me as pretty intelligent."

"He is, but…" She looked disheartened, and that bothered Trey more than he wanted to admit. What she was asking was nonetheless unreasonable.

"But?"

"I don't want him using it as an excuse for not setting high goals and doing his best. Dave's wanted to go into the military since he was a kid," she said. "He took the tests for the academies and got excellent ratings—"

"But couldn't pass the physical."

She nodded. "He's says now he doesn't even want to go to college, that he has no idea what to major in."

"He doesn't have to decide that now, not yet."

"He's discouraged, thinks no one will give him a job—"

"Of course they will."

She sighed. "There are some things he may never be able to do, like military service—"

"And driving a car?"

She studied him with annoyance.

"Eventually he'll get a license. First he has to be sure his disorder is fully under control, so he isn't a threat to himself or anyone else on the road."

"He said he hasn't had a seizure in two years."

"Almost two years. When he turns eighteen he'll be able to get a license without my permission. In the meantime he has to focus on the things he can do, not the things he can't."

"Nicole," Trey said quietly, "I can't imagine why you think I could help him give up his primary ambition. I'm a NASCAR driver, which is all I've ever wanted to be. I don't see how I can inspire him when—"

"Talk to him, Trey, that's all I'm asking. The nature of

your epilepsy is different from his, but the underlying disorder is the same. Besides, he doesn't want to be a NASCAR driver—"

"Of course he does!" Trey arched back, aghast. What she was saying was heresy. "Everybody wants to be a NASCAR driver."

She raised her eyebrows, the twinkle came back to her eyes, then broke into a smile to match his. It amazed him how it lifted his spirits, sent a pleasant electrical impulse to his fevered brain—and other parts of his anatomy.

"Your humility is inspiring, too," she purred.

He grinned. "That's me, Humble Trey. Hmm, I may have to talk to Gaby Colson about using that as my new moniker. Humble Trey. Has a ring to it, don't you think? Humble Trey won at Daytona today but declined praise for the achievement, claiming it was a lucky gust of wind produced by cheering fans that pushed him over the finish line."

She laughed. "Keep this up and you won't be humble very long. Not only that, but your nose will grow and get in the way of the steering wheel."

He chuckled. "Gee, knocked off my pedestal already."

"So how about it?" she asked before he could fully recover.

He was still enjoying the happy sparks in her delightful blue eyes. "How about what?"

"Telling Dave you—"

He sobered. "Persistent. I have to admire that, even when it's used against me."

"I'm not against you."

Oh, but how he wished she were. The idea of taking her in his arms and pressing her body against his was enough to short-circuit his entire nervous system.

He had forced his thoughts back to the present situation, to Dave Foster rather than Nicole Foster. Tough to do with her sitting right there in front of him, within touching distance; might as well try to shoot from forty-third to first in one lap.

Focus, where were his thoughts supposed to be? Oh, yeah, Dave. Her brother. He liked the tall, lanky teenager and could sympathize with his frustration. They were more than a dozen years apart in age, but not so many he couldn't remember what it was like to feel hemmed in by rules and expectations. Both of his brothers were older. Maybe this was his opportunity to have a kid brother of his own. Besides, if he became a mentor to the teenager he'd no doubt have to spend more time with his CFS, perhaps explore her compulsive nature more closely.

"I'll make a deal with you," he said. "I'll talk to Dave about my seizure disorder on the condition that he sign an affidavit promising not to disclose it to anyone."

"That's reasonable," she said reluctantly. "I suppose putting it in writing makes sense, too—"

"What's more," Trey pressed on, "you will have to countersign it as his legal guardian."

"That won't be necessary, Trey. I'm already bound by medical confidentiality."

"Let me make myself perfectly clear," he said, uncrossing his legs. "I'm not worried about *you* violating medical ethics. This document will hold you personally responsible for anything *Dave* might say about my situation."

Her mouth fell open. "That's blackmail," she sputtered when she finally found her voice.

"Hardly. I'm not forcing you or your brother to do anything or threatening to do anything against either of you if you don't sign it. I'm merely protecting *my* interests, legally and ethically. If you're not sure you want to accept that kind of responsibility or if you're not one hundred percent confident that your brother will protect *your* interests, don't sign it. That's fine with me. We'll end the discussion with no hard feelings."

He watched her during the long pause that followed. Anger and confusion, definitely. Her eyebrows drew together. Her hands twitched on the counter. For a second, maybe even rage. He was afraid she was going to bolt. That would solve the epilepsy crisis, but it would also end any chance of getting to know her better, and he did want to know her better.

"I…" She gaped at him. He could practically see the uncertainty whirling inside her head, that stuck-in-a-corner confusion. He didn't suppose she was normally an indecisive woman, but she was now.

He'd thrown her for a loop. He didn't like destabilizing her world. His instinct was to do the opposite, to protect her peace of mind, to support her.

She ignored him for three solid minutes. It seemed even longer, but he didn't interrupt her or make a move that might suggest impatience. At one point he doubted she was fully conscious of him being there. Humbling, he thought with a thin smile. Humble Trey.

At last she said, "It's a deal."

It was his turn to be surprised. He hadn't been sure she'd go along with his proposal. In fact he'd half expected her to throw him out. Her anger would have disturbed him. Her turning down the deal wouldn't have.

"Fax me the papers," she said, standing up.

"I don't want to take a chance on anyone else seeing them. I'll have them hand couriered in a sealed envelope," he said. "Better yet…" He came up to her, placed his hands on her shoulders, drew her slowly closer and wrapped his arms around her, then brought his mouth down to hers and kissed her. He could feel her stiffen, hesitate, then she relaxed. Not completely but enough to signal she wasn't opposed to being kissed. When she met him halfway, he closed his eyes and savored the taste of her. The moment didn't last, however. She eased herself out of his arms. "Better yet," he repeated, his voice husky, "I'll deliver the papers myself."

NICOLE SAT AT HER DESK with mixed emotions. She'd achieved her goal of getting Trey to help her brother focus on the positive rather than the negative, but something had happened in the process, something she didn't understand. She was seeing a different aspect of Trey Sanford. Not just the dedicated NASCAR driver or the flirt who had women trailing after him—even across international borders, if the blogs could be believed—but a serious businessman, as well. Her brother would learn that one of his heroes shared his affliction, and that the guy knew how to cover his back, a valuable lesson.

But it wasn't her brother who was foremost in her mind as she drove home that afternoon. It was the man she'd recruited to help him. She'd underestimated Trey Sanford, she realized. He'd surprised her with the paper for Dave to sign, though it was a reasonable enough request, but having her countersign it…what did it mean? That he didn't trust Dave, or that he didn't trust her?

It was a test, and she wasn't sure if she'd passed or failed it. One thing she'd learned was that Trey Sanford was a strong man. Strong in the sense that he knew how to protect himself, and strong in the way he had let her make up her own mind. He could have tried to influence her decision when she stared at the wall, but he let her weigh the situation for herself. She liked that. She liked being in the presence of his strength and not feeling threatened by it. She liked his ability to be both forthright and lighthearted, to not take himself too seriously—

Humble Trey indeed!—and yet not compromise on principle.

As for being in his presence… She liked that more than she wanted to admit. He stirred something in her, a tension that aroused her senses, an awareness of herself as a woman, of him as a man.

She'd been hoping that he would kiss her. When they'd gotten into their discussion, which was closer to a dispute, about his epilepsy, she was sure the opportunity had been lost.

Then he had kissed her anyway.

She smiled. He was a good kisser.

A few hours later, she received a phone call from Trey.

"I have the paperwork ready," he said. "Are you still sure you want to go through with this?"

"Of course. That was fast."

After a slight pause he asked, "You still mad at me?"

She almost remarked that he sounded like Humble Trey, the way he asked the question. Humble Trey made her laugh, but the strong, assertive, even domineering man she'd had to deal with did other things to her, as well, things she wanted to experience more of.

"I'm not mad at you. You caught me off guard, that's all. I wasn't expecting… What about the paperwork? How do you want to handle it?"

"I thought I'd bring it by and answer any questions you or your brother might have. Both of you can sign it, if you still want to, and we can go from there."

"When?"

"Tonight, at your house?"

She worked at the free clinic in neighboring Hendersonville on Monday and Tuesday afternoons and evenings. It was short notice but she'd trade shifts with John Preston. The pediatrician normally worked there on Wednesday nights.

"Let me give you the address."

"I know where you live." She could hear the playfulness in his voice and it surprised her how reassuring it was.

"Oh, yes, I forgot you drove Dave home. About five o'clock?"

"I'll see you then."

CHAPTER FIVE

THE HOUSE WAS RIGHT out of *Southern Living,* sophisticated and charming. Hanging baskets of brilliantly colored begonias and petunias dotted the front porch. Hostas and ornamental black currants lined the flower beds at the base of the porch; a rock garden danced around the trunk of a giant oak tree lending its variegated color to the genteel scene.

Trey parked in the semicircular driveway and climbed the six steps to the colonnaded porch. He was reaching for the bell when the door opened and Dave smiled down at him. They shook hands.

"Sis told me you were coming. She came home early and is in the kitchen fixing tea." He closed the door behind them and led Trey to the left into the living room, which fully matched expectations. Floral-patterned slipcovers brightened comfortable-looking overstuffed furniture. The rug on the polished maple floor appeared to be old but in good condition. The cold fireplace had shiny brass and-irons. Above the white mantel hung an oil seascape in an ornate gilt frame.

Nicole joined them carrying a tray with a frosty pitcher and three glasses.

"You haven't told him the reason for my visit?" Trey asked, as she set the tray on the coffee table and started pouring the beverage into the ice-filled glasses. Her movements weren't intentionally provocative. On the contrary, it was their unconsciously natural grace, so feminine, that entranced him and stirred his blood.

She handed him a sweaty glass. Their fingers touched fleetingly. He felt their warmth. "I figured I'd leave it to you," she said.

Trey explained to Dave that what he was about to tell him was so sensitive that Dave had to promise to keep it confidential. He couldn't tell anyone about it under any circumstances, and he had to avoid discussing it even with his sister if they were in a place where they could be overheard.

Dave turned to his sister. "Do you know what he's talking about?"

She nodded. "We made a deal. You pledge in writing to maintain his confidence, I'll sign, as well, to back it up, and we'll go on from there."

"That won't be necessary, the paperwork, I mean," said Trey.

"But—" Nicole looked both pleased and bewildered.

"I trust you," he said. "If I can't count on your word, a piece of paper won't make any difference."

Dave appeared even more confused then before. "So what's this big secret?"

Trey told him. "I have epilepsy."

Dave stared at him. "You're sh—kidding me."

Trey shook his head.

Nicole finished pouring the tea and handed it around.

"Not exactly like yours. I have what are called absence seizures," Trey explained, "the kind where I seem to zone out."

"Do you ever have convulsions?" Dave asked.

"No, just daydream states, where I sort of go into a trance."

"Have you always had them?"

"Mine started when I was sixteen. I was on the high

school football team. We were playing against Central. Hoagie Milford threw a forward pass. I was on the twelve-yard line and caught it in midair, came down, and a linebacker from Central plowed into me like an eighteen-wheeler on a downhill slope. At least, that's what they tell me. I don't remember any of it. They said I was out for nearly five minutes. I was rushed to the hospital, of course. No bones broken. I didn't even have any bruises that really counted, but I did have a mild concussion. They kept me in the hospital for a day, then sent me home. No big deal, right?"

Trey took a sip of his tea, decided he was thirsty and downed half of it in three gulps.

"A couple of weeks after that I had my first episode. Nobody knew what to make of it at the time. We were having dinner at home. I stopped eating, just sat there. My brother Brent asked me to pass something to him. I didn't do it, didn't do anything. My mother repeated the request and I still didn't respond. My brother Adam waved his hand in front of my face and I didn't react. Then I snapped out of it as if nothing had happened.

"Everybody laughed. They thought I had been playing a joke. All I could do was grin. I didn't want to admit I didn't have a clue what they were talking about. The second time it happened I was out in the garage at home, helping my father tune the engine of a forty-nine Packard he and Brent were restoring. I went to the workbench to get a tool he'd asked for, stopped and stood there without moving a muscle for a couple of minutes, then I snapped out of it as if nothing had happened. When Dad and Brent told me about it, I didn't believe them, because for me there had been no interruption."

"Didn't your dad realize something was wrong?" Dave asked.

"He hadn't been there the first time, and no one had told him about it. Like I said, everybody thought I was clowning around. This time Dad figured I was daydreaming, not paying attention."

"Were you aware of being out of it? I mean, did everything go into slow motion?"

"Nope. I've had a few episodes like that, but usually it's a slice of time gone missing. I can be jarred out of it, if the people around me understand what's going on. The third time it happened, I was getting ready to drive in a regional series race. A few minutes before start-up I went for a drink of water and stood at the water fountain, my finger on the button, frozen in place. My father yelled to me to get a move on. I remained perfectly still. Finally he came up to me, got in my face. I still didn't react. He was royally ticked. 'Stop playing games,' he yelled in my ear, but I didn't do anything. Finally, he shook me. Pretty hard. It wasn't like him, by the way. You've no doubt heard stories about Wild Bobby Sanford, and most of them are probably true, but he wasn't a violent man."

Trey didn't often talk about his dad, who had been an SOB in many ways. He couldn't defend the things his father had done, especially his philandering, but the old man had had a good side, too. People tended to forget that, although remarkably his mother hadn't.

"Anyway, he shook me out of that seizure."

"Did you race?" Dave asked.

"He wouldn't let me. He was mad as hell but not at me. Dad was… I had a good record till then and was favored to win that day. Canceling at the last minute wasn't something anyone liked doing, but Dad understood something was seriously wrong, and he couldn't take a chance on me getting hurt or hurting somebody else."

"What reason did he give for you dropping out?" Nicole asked.

Trey laughed. "Food poisoning. Said I must have eaten something that didn't agree with me and that I was indisposed."

"What about you? Did you understand what was going on?"

"Not really. I could remember my father shaking me. I didn't know why or how we'd gotten to that point. I'd probably had other episodes nobody knew about, occasions when I seemed to misplace little pieces of time."

"How much time?"

"Not hours, minutes."

"Was it scary?" asked Dave.

"Sure it was. I didn't understand what was going on. That's always scary."

"So what happened then?" Nicole asked.

"Mom insisted I get medical help. Dad wasn't ready to admit there was anything seriously wrong, but she put her foot down and took me to the family doctor, who ran the usual tests, including an EKG, but he couldn't find anything wrong. He suggested it might be a seizure disorder. 'What's that?' Dad asked. When the doctor said 'epilepsy,' Dad turned white as a sheet. I guess he was conjuring up the usual stereotypes, frothing at the mouth and all that nonsense. The doctor explained it wasn't like that, that it was a neurological disorder, like diabetes is an organ disorder. Mom asked the usual questions. What caused it? Was there a cure? The doctor said the blow to the head might have caused it or it might have triggered a preexisting condition. There was no way of knowing. That wasn't the answer Dad wanted to hear. As for a cure…there were certain treatments, ranging from medication to surgery, but we'd have to go to a specialist to find out if any of them was appropriate."

"But you have been cured?" Dave stated, optimistic hope hanging in his words.

"The condition is under control, but it's still there." Trey took a slug of his iced tea. "Like I said, I was driving in one of NASCAR's regional series at the time and doing pretty well. Dad was convinced I was headed for the NASCAR Sprint Cup Series, but he also knew if word got out that I'd had any sort of seizure, even if it turned out I didn't have epilepsy, my career would be over before it got started. After Dad died and I'd proven myself, my brothers and I discussed it with Mom. We decided the admission would just raise more questions, especially since I was going to Mexico for treatment."

"Why are you?"

"Dad was afraid if he took me to a specialist here in the States word would get out and—"

"He didn't trust American medical institutions to maintain patient confidentiality?" Nicole sounded both aghast and personally insulted.

Trey shook his head. "He wasn't worried about medical people. It was the press he feared. Dad was…well, I think you know he was sort of a flamboyant figure. The paparazzi were always dogging his heels and mine and my brothers', for that matter. Dad was sure if he took me to a local neurologist the news would spread, so he shopped around in different parts of the country. Then he found Dr. Denise Price, an American pediatric neurologist specializing in seizure disorders, in Mexico. He could fly me there in our private plane without anybody being the wiser."

"And that's what you did?" Dave asked.

"Yep. Dad died shortly after that, but my mother insisted I keep going and my brothers have been absolutely great. Brent is a pilot—he runs his own private charter service now—and he flew me down whenever I needed, until I got a private pilot's license myself a couple of years ago."

"I'm surprised you were able to obtain FAA approval," Nicole commented. "Actually, I'm surprised NASCAR lets you drive."

"The FAA required a certificate from my doctor verifying that I hadn't had a seizure in at least two years, that I was receiving treatment to minimize the risk of seizures, and that the medication I was taking wasn't in itself an impediment to flying a plane. As for NASCAR," Trey added, "a select number of officials are aware of my condition, have reviewed the data and approved of me driving. They also agree it's in my best interest and theirs that it be kept confidential, which is why I considered having you sign the agreement."

"How long has it been since you've had a seizure?" Dave asked.

"Almost six years."

"Wow. What kind of medication are you taking?"

Trey named it.

"That's it? That stuff is nothing. I have to take it and three other pills that are a lot stronger twice a day."

"I've been able to reduce my meds," Trey continued, "because six years ago Dr. Price implanted a Vagus Nerve Stimulator in my chest." He explained what a VNS was and how it functioned. "It's not suitable for all patients, and it's not a cure but a treatment. Some people still have to take heavy medication, others experience adverse side effects, like sore throats, throat pain, even changes in their voices, especially when the device is active. I've been fortunate. I haven't run into any of those problems. Tell me about your seizures," he said to Dave.

The lanky teenager frowned. "They're called tonic-clonic. They're convulsions, and they can be pretty bad, what people who don't understand call fits."

"How often do you have them?"

"I used to have them a lot, sometimes several times a day."

"They were especially bad right after our parents died," Nicole pointed out. "It took a long time to adjust his medication."

"But I haven't had a seizure in nearly two years," said Dave.

"Sounds like you have everything under control," Trey said.

"Some control," Dave complained with a twist of his mouth. "The stuff I have to take…sometimes it makes me really groggy. Other times I feel like I'm wired, sort of tripped out. I hate it."

Trey understood. He'd had similar problems with his oral medication initially, and his seizures were relatively benign, not nearly as dramatic as Dave's. It was miserable trying to function in a pea-soup fog.

He also realized Nicole was probably correct in not wanting her brother to drive. Without strong medication Dave was subject to violent seizures. With it, he was doped up. Either alternative put him and everyone else on the road at risk. Trey sympathized with the kid.

"Do you understand now why I've been so secretive?"

"Yeah," Dave acknowledged. "People don't understand epilepsy."

Trey agreed. "I don't want other drivers afraid of being on the track with me, and fans…well, you can imagine. Every time I made a mistake or was involved in an accident, they'd be asking if I had a seizure, if that's why I crashed."

This, of course, was precisely what Nicole had done.

He glanced her way to find her staring at her hands folded in her lap and felt a little tug of sympathy for her. Then she surprised him by reaching over and taking his hand in hers. For that split second when her skin first made contact with his he thought his heart would stop. Instead it pounded double-time. He squeezed her fingers in return.

"At least you can drive a car," Dave said. "I'm not even allowed to play football or other contact sports or do anything that's considered violent."

"You're a champion swimmer," Nicole reminded him. "You have a wall full of medals and awards upstairs."

"Swimmer, huh?" Trey smiled. "That explains those broad shoulders. I wondered if you might be a bodybuilder."

Another shrug, but it was plain the kid was pleased with the compliment.

"Hey, don't brush it off lightly. There are plenty of people who can't swim, and there are even more of us who don't win medals at it."

The younger man didn't seem appeased.

"Look, Dave," Trey went on, "do I wish I didn't have epilepsy? Of course I do, but it isn't a moral issue. We do what we're good at, and we work to make ourselves better. Everybody has limitations."

"You don't."

Trey laughed. "Don't kid yourself. There are a ton of things I can't do or can't do well. Music, for instance. I'd give anything to be able to play a musical instrument. My complete lack of talent has nothing to do with epilepsy. Don't let a handicap in one area cripple you from accomplishing things in others. Your sister tells me you're a straight-A student but that you're questioning whether to go to college now since you didn't get accepted by a service academy. I think that would be a mistake. Getting an education is important whether you march to class in uniform or stroll there in jeans. Your brain may go haywire once in a while, but your doctor will help keep it under control with meds. What you do with the rest of your time is up to you alone."

"But what am I going to study?"

"Go to school and find out. That's what freshman year is all about. But if you don't look, you'll never find it." He was beginning to sound like a lecturer, Trey realized, and the kid didn't need that. To his relief, Dave didn't seem to be annoyed. He'd probably heard the same thing from his CFS, but Trey knew what qualified him as an expert— being from out of town.

The grandfather clock in the hall struck six.

Dave climbed to his feet. "Jenny will wonder what's happened to me. We're playing again tonight. We want to get to the shop early to tune up and practice." He came over to Trey, who also rose. The two men shook hands. "You don't have to worry about me. Your secret's safe." He turned to his sister. "After the session tonight I'm going with Jenny to her place. I can walk home from there. I'll be back around ten. Make that eleven. Thanks for coming over and telling me," he told Trey.

"Sorry about the cloak-and-dagger stuff."

Dave laughed. "Forget it. Heck, in your position I'd do the same thing. In fact, in your position I probably wouldn't even have told me."

As Nicole and Trey stood side by side between the couches watching her brother run out the front door, she slipped her hand in his.

CHAPTER SIX

"I APOLOGIZE FOR MY brother running out on you like that."

Trey chuckled softly and squeezed her hand. "Hey, there's a girl involved." He shifted so they were face-to-face and only a few inches apart. "I understand that." He rested his free hand on her hip, their joined hands between them. "Dave's a good kid. You can be proud of the job you've done raising him."

"Sometimes I wonder."

"Spoken like a true parent," he muttered and kissed her sweetly on her slightly puckered mouth.

Those beautiful clear blue eyes widened in shock, but he saw pleasure there, too, and if he was correctly reading the quivering of her soft lips against his, hunger, as well.

Seconds passed before she pulled back, time enough for him to catch the intrigue in her shy glance as she turned away from him. He was both pleased and amused by the discomfort he'd instigated. A sugary little kiss for now, sweetness he wouldn't mind tasting again, exploring, making more spicy.

"Thanks for encouraging him."

It took him a moment to corral his brain. She was talking about her brother.

"He's going to be fine, Nicci. He's—"

"Nicci?" Her eyes widened and sparkled. "Nobody ever calls me Nicci."

"No?" He grinned. "Good. It'll be my special name for you. One I use in private when the two of us are alone, Nicci." He was probably making a fool of himself, but she didn't laugh, didn't huff, didn't pull away. He kissed her again, more intimately this time, drawing her tighter against his body.

A pleased smile curled the corners of her mouth. Suddenly she seemed to understand the effect she was having on him and let out a derisive chuckle, went over to the coffee table, lifted the pitcher and refilled his tea glass.

"Thanks again for leveling with Dave and for not making us sign anything."

"I got my point across."

She retrieved her drink and settled into the easy chair she'd previously occupied. He resumed his place on the opposing couch. They stared at each other.

He hadn't done it for Dave, though he hoped the talk would do the kid some good. He'd done it for her, because she was searching for a way to help her brother, like any good parent. She was exactly the kind of woman he wanted as the mother of his children.

"In spite of everything, epilepsy and the death of your father," she said, "you've lived a remarkably charmed life?"

He'd never thought of himself in those terms, but of course it was true. He'd never wanted financially and he was in a high-profile profession that was exciting and envied. Still, was fame and fortune all there was? Hardly. His mother had possessed both and until recent years would hardly have called her life charmed, and his brother Brent's experience demonstrated how fickle good fortune could be. He'd been at the top of his game as a driver when an accusation was made against him that he'd sabotaged Kent Grosso's car. Brent had maintained his innocence, still did, but he'd walked away from a promising career rather than keep up the fight. A mistake, in Trey's judgment.

He took in the room he was sitting in, its rich furnishings, the gilt-framed oil paintings on the walls, the Oriental carpets on the floors, and wanted to remind Nicole she hadn't fared too poorly, either.

"This is a beautiful house," he noted instead. "Have you lived here long?"

"My entire life," she replied before her eyes narrowed fleetingly in recognition of the underlying message. "Would you like to see the rest of it?"

He nodded. House tours weren't normally high on his list of things to do. "If you'll guide me."

She led him into the dining room. The glistening dark wood table had a lace runner down its length. The crystal chandelier sparkled with a dozen flickering electric candles. The armchair seats were upholstered in satiny stripes. Between wide French windows stood a marble fireplace, its hearth at floor level, logs artistically arranged behind shiny brass andirons.

The kitchen beyond the swinging door was modest in size, the polished wood cabinets custom-made, the countertops granite, the appliances stainless steel.

Rather than return to the hallway, Nicole led him up the narrow back stairs. Three small stained-glass windows escalated the outside wall. They emerged on the second floor. The ceiling, even here, was high, with elaborate cove molding and medallions over the chandelier suspended above the central stairwell.

"Master suite on the right," Nicole explained. "On the left three bedrooms. Dave uses the rear bedroom—I don't think you want to see that."

Trey snickered. "A teenager's room, eh? What about the master suite?"

Her hesitation and the sudden shyness in her eyes spoke volumes. He wanted to see her bedroom, her private space, her intimate retreat. She was pleased yet reticent. "Sure."

They crossed the hall. She threw open the double doors and stood back. He stepped into a sitting room that was neat and orderly and out of another age. He made his way toward the single doorway to the adjoining room.

Her bed was big, its canopy nearly reaching the ceiling. The matching bedside tables, dresser, highboy and vanity were richly polished dark wood. The old-fashioned decor seemed at odds with the young woman he'd bantered with at a NASCAR race, yet there was something about the contrasting images that simultaneously intrigued and excited him. This, Trey realized, was her retreat, a world in the past where there were no surprises but that could contain memories and romance.

He pictured her in a diaphanous negligee, propped up on the enormous pillows, smiling at him, beckoning him.

Whew. Down, boy, down.

She gazed at him, her blue eyes twinkling, as if she could read his mind. "There's one other room I'd like to show you."

They descended the main staircase.

At the bottom, instead of turning right into the living room, she motioned him down the hall to the left. From outside the door it looked like another sitting room—a couple of wingback chairs separated by a table with a Tiffany lamp. Once he stepped inside, however, he saw it differently. Three walls of dark-stained bookcases. What was even more impressive was that they were filled with mostly leather-bound volumes, some in sets, others of varying sizes, ranging from small handbooks to quarto-size tomes.

"Wow!"

She smiled. "Dad was a reader. It was one of the things that drew him and my mom together. When he was over in Europe he found several collections of old books, bought them and sent them home. Here in the States he pursued what had become an active hobby." She extended her arm in a broad sweep. "This is the result."

Trey approached what appeared to be the oldest volumes and scanned the titles. Adam Smith. Samuel Johnson, John Dryden, William Blake. "First editions?"

"Some of them. I'm considering donating them to the local college."

"Have you read any of them?"

She made an ironic sound. "I've read all of them, but in modern editions, because I didn't want to handle these for fear of damaging them."

"Sort of defeats the purpose, doesn't it?"

She laughed good-naturedly. "Not if you're a collector. You don't actually use the books and manuals that you collect, do you?"

"I would, if I had the vehicles they correspond to, but you're right. I probably wouldn't. I'd make copies and use them instead. Don't have to worry about grease stains on pages that way. Are you still adding to the collection?"

"I haven't had much of a chance the past few years. With medical training out of the way and Dave going off to college soon, maybe I will now."

They could go book hunting together, he thought, wander through shops. He could peer over her shoulder when she found a new treasure and share the joy of the quiet adventure with her. He imagined them sitting in the evening reading, aware of each other, and that awareness leading them to explore other experiences.

He took a deep breath. "Dave said your father was a doctor. I guess it was natural for you, then, to go into medicine."

She nodded. "Pretty much. My grandfather, too. Like you and NASCAR. For as long as I can remember I've wanted to be a doctor. As a kid I used to go with my father sometimes when he made house calls. Occasionally I had to wait in the car, but mostly I was allowed to go in with him and meet people. Sometimes there wasn't much he could do for his patients but console them and try to relieve their pain, but he was always greeted as a positive force in their lives. I wanted to do that, too."

An idealist, Trey thought. "I don't imagine you spent all your time studying medical books. What kind of hobbies did you have growing up?"

She relaxed into a wingback near a writing desk. "Athletics runs in the family, too. My grandfather played football in college and stayed physically active his entire life. Walked three miles a day and lived to be ninety. My parents competed in golf and tennis tournaments. We all played volleyball and water-skied in the summer, ice-skated and skied in the winter. As far back as elementary school I got hooked on running. Dad was sure I was going to be in the Olympics."

Trey turned from the stack of books he was examining. "Were you?" he pictured her in a sleek, shiny running suit, her long muscular legs slicing through the air, arms pumping, her chest heaving. Oh, yeah.

She smiled. "Didn't make the cut, but I did compete in track in high school and college."

He'd hated running in high school, but it was part of football training. Maybe if she had been a cheerleader, he could have talked her into pacing him. He had no doubt she could have talked him into doing anything. Maybe she still could.

"I considered delaying medical school for a few years to pursue the Olympic dream, then my folks were killed in a private plane crash. Dave was almost ten and having serious problems with his seizures at the time. I put aside my athletic ambitions and dropped out of medical school for a year to assume full guardianship of him. He needed a stable home more than ever."

"You've had a rough time of it," Trey observed.

"He's my brother," she replied without a hint of self-pity or regret. "We're family. That always comes first."

A woman who had a mind of her own, a woman with determination and dedication. His imagination captured her tall, slender figure in skimpy running shorts, long legs sinewy with muscle, arms pumping, eyes sparkling at the victory line strung out ahead. Him standing behind the ribbon, ready to catch her.

The clock in the hallway struck three-quarters of the hour. "Are you going to Dave's jam session?"

"You bet. I rarely get a chance because I work at the clinic on Tuesday evenings."

"What about tonight?"

"I traded shifts with one of my colleagues."

"To be with me? Ah, gee, I'm flattered."

She laughed. "What an ego."

"Well, didn't you?"

She put a finger to the corner of her mouth. "I suppose you could say that."

"Okay, I will." He gave her a peck on the forehead. "What about dinner? You haven't eaten yet, have you?"

She shook her head. "I thought I'd pick up something on the way home. Would you like to join me? Fast food, I'm afraid. If your ego can take it, that is."

"You think I'm a snob?"

"Let's say you're from another world."

"Otherworldly. I like that. I think."

She snickered. "So how about it? Join me?"

He had several replies for that but settled on, "Yes."

They took Trey's car, arrived at the music shop as the first musical chords were being struck, but the only chairs available were on opposite sides of the long, narrow room. Halfway through the third or fourth number, Nicole got up and walked out, extracting her cell phone—she'd put it on vibrate—from her pocket. Trey followed and watched the expression on her face change from curious to intense. Instantly he realized *Dr.* Foster had all but forgotten him.

"Yes, of course," she said. "How many? I'm on my way. Better contact Dr. Langhorne, too. Okay, good. Also check with anesthesiology and see if they need augmentation. It's going to be a long night." She clicked off the phone and stared at Trey. "A rain check on dinner? Sorry. That was the hospital. An eighteen-wheeler skidded off a mountain road and rolled into a house below it. So far casualties have been limited to a few adults with broken bones, but it's about to get worse. There were six kids in the house, and they haven't been able to dig them out yet."

CHAPTER SEVEN

"Do you want me to take you directly to the hospital?" Trey asked.

"No." Her answer was decisive. Clearly she was in doctor mode. "I need to pick up my car. Our place is on the way, so there won't be more than a minute or two delay."

"What about dinner?"

He'd been looking forward to sharing a bucket of chicken or whatever she decided on. The fare didn't make any difference. The important thing was her company. His appetite kept toying with possible after-dinner activities.

She shook her head. "Another time. This will be an all-nighter. I'll grab a bite when I can at the clinic, like everybody else."

He was tempted to hang around. He had his wireless laptop with him. E-mails from his crew chief, his publicist and representatives of several sponsors were no doubt stacking up, but medical facilities frowned on the use of electronic devices in their buildings, so he'd end up sitting in his car. Staying to be near Nicole would be futile. He also had a long day ahead of him tomorrow and a two-hour drive home tonight.

"I'll see you this weekend at Dover, won't I?" Trey asked on the drive to her house.

"Afraid not. Dr. Halsey, the orthopedist I've been filling in for, will be back on the job."

"Come on your own, then. I can have tickets and passes available for you at the will-call window. You'll be able to watch the race from the stands or the pit area instead of on a monitor in the infield care center. Much more exciting."

"I know, and I'd love to be there, but last weekend put an extra workload on my colleagues at the clinic. Payback time."

"Surely they'd understand—"

"That I had other medical opportunities to pursue? They've been very supportive, but we share a medical practice. This would be social, not professional. I have to pull my load."

He reached over and squeezed her hand. "I'm disappointed that I won't get to see you. Suppose I dislocate my shoulder again?"

"Oh, you'll like Dr. Halsey," she assured him, as though he'd been serious. "He's much more experienced than I am, has an excellent reputation—"

"Hardly the same." He continued to hold her hand beneath his. "He can never do for me what you do."

He glanced over and saw her eyes sparkling at him. "We're not talking about joint alignment, are we?"

He stared at the road ahead, trying to keep a straight face, then broke into a grin. "What do you think?"

She reversed her hand so it was palm to palm with his. Her grip was soft, warm, tantalizingly feminine. The way his pulse was picking up he probably ought to disengage and drag the magnetized band on his right wrist across his VNS to be on the safe side, but he instantly rejected the idea. There was no way he could space out with her touching him.

He started to turn into the round driveway in front of her house, but she directed him to take the long pavement leading to the garage behind it. He came to a stop in front of the left-hand pull-down door. Before she had time to extract herself from the low seat, he'd climbed out his side of the sports car and was extending his hand. Instead of releasing her when she stood, however, he pulled her against him.

He knew she was anxious to be on her way, but she didn't resist when he brushed his lips against hers, withdrew, then pressed them against hers in a way that left no doubt of his feelings. The kiss lingered innocently for a few more seconds, then they each deepened it into more intimate contact. When, at last, she pulled away a minute later, they were both breathing heavily.

She rested her head against his chest. "Sorry about dinner. I was looking forward to dessert, too."

"You're a devil," he said in near despair. "I hadn't even thought about dessert."

"Liar." She laughed and pressed the remote she'd extracted from her purse. The garage door grumbled its way up.

"Is there anything I can do?" he asked.

She touched his cheek with her fingertips. "Thanks for asking, but frankly you'd be in the way—and a distraction. Maybe after we get things sorted out you can visit some of the victims. I'm sure they'd love to have a famous NASCAR driver show up." She gave him a quick peck on the cheek. "I've got to run."

She dashed to her car and seconds later was backing out. He rubbed his right wrist across his upper chest as he listened to her car tear down the driveway and turn onto the street with a screech of tires. Suddenly the world around him was dead silent. Shaking his head, he climbed back into his car and restarted the engine. Reversing direction, he stared up at the dark eaves of the back of the house, at the faint glow of a light left on in the master suite upstairs. His mind pictured the canopied bed, the sea of pillows against the headboard. The evening hadn't ended the way he would have liked it to—he hoped the emergency turned out to be less critical than it sounded—but overall he wasn't displeased. He'd kissed her and she'd kissed him back a second time.

NICOLE WAS EVER AMAZED at the resilience of the human body and the human spirit. What had promised to be a devastating night turned into one of extraordinary heroism and hope. The children in the smashed house were trapped there, but the eldest of them, a girl of fourteen, who had been babysitting the other five, had possessed the maturity and presence of mind to keep them talking and even singing. She later admitted she suspected one of them was seriously hurt because she could smell blood, but she refused to let them consider the possibility that it was anything more than a minor cut or scratch. Fortunately it wasn't, but she had no way of knowing that in the darkness of the tiny cavity that had been created when the room they were in collapsed like an accordion.

It took four hours for the rescue team to reach them. One worker in the process got his leg caught in a vise when a rafter shifted and pinned him. He required several hours of surgery, but Nicole was able to put the pieces back together with a combination of screws and superglue.

It was already daylight when she returned to the old Victorian house. An hour after arriving at the hospital the night before she had tried to call Dave on his cell phone, but he'd turned it off for his bluegrass session. She'd left a message that she probably wouldn't be home for several hours, maybe all night. It wouldn't be the first time, but this was a first for her to open the front door, step inside after a marathon session and not be thinking of her bed. Not directly, at least. As she passed the library, she pictured Trey standing among the rows of books, enthralled by their rarity and quality, which led her to think about the rarity and quality of the kiss they had shared.

She mounted the stairs alone. Not exactly what she'd had in mind twelve hours earlier.

TREY WASN'T HAVING A good day. His brother Adam, the owner of Sanford Racing, had been on his back from the moment he returned his multiple calls Tuesday night.

"Where the hell have you been?" Adam had demanded. "I was finally able to set up a meeting with Alley Cat Products for late this afternoon—"

"If you'd told me beforehand," Trey countered, "I would have hung around. I went up into the mountains for a few hours. Cell-phone reception up there is lousy." In fact, he'd turned it off when he'd gone to see Nicole and Dave and had forgotten to power it up again.

"Ethan's been trying to reach you, too, about some engine modifications his engine builder wants to install."

"I'll call him right after I hang up on you." There was a moment of silence. Trey realized his brother couldn't tell if he was being literal or sarcastic. "As soon as I get off the phone with you," he clarified.

"We've got to do better," Adam reminded him. Translation: *you* have to do better. "As a result of Sunday's DNF, we're now in seventeenth place and more than four hundred points behind the leader. Unless we move up quickly, we don't have a chance of making the Chase for the NASCAR Sprint Cup."

Trey started to reply, to assure him things would improve, but his brother wasn't in listening mode.

"At least those rumors about you having a girl down in Mexico have died down. There've been enough distractions about the family without that subject coming up again."

He paused, giving Trey an opportunity to confirm his statement, but Trey chose to remain silent. The *woman* who was distracting him wasn't an imaginary one in Mexico but a very real flesh-and-blood redhead in Brevard, North Carolina. He wondered even now how she was handling the medical emergency she'd been called out on and wished he'd stayed. He could have lent the victims and their families his moral support and, when the crisis was over, taken Nicole somewhere to eat—probably breakfast—then home. What happened there… Breakfast didn't usually come with dessert, but…

"You still there?" Adam asked.

"I'm still here," Trey said. "Forget about the rumor mill. You know as well as I do that any response serves only to feed it. You, Ethan and Gaby know the score. That's all that matters."

"What matters is that you start winning."

"Gee, why didn't I think of that," Trey shot back. "You finished? If you are, we can hang up and I can call Ethan and straighten things out with him. I'll see you tomorrow at the garage." He disconnected without waiting for a reply.

The worst part for Trey was that Adam was right. His record for the season was rocky. He'd make the top ten—or get a DNF. Nothing consistent. Sponsors and fans would forgive slumps, but when did a slump cease to be an anomaly and become a pattern of poor performance?

Wednesday morning he went into the garage and did his best to cheer people up, constantly looking at the bright side. For the first time he got the feeling that his team members were patronizing him, laughing at his quips and agreeing with his optimistic assessments but not believing them. He had a crisis of confidence on his hands, and he had to be the one to cure it.

Thursday the team deployed to Dover. On the surface everything was progressing smoothly, but Trey could feel the undercurrent, the doubt that they would do well…that *he could* do well. What exactly had he done to merit this suspicion? True, there had been missteps, wrong moves, miscalculations. He'd occasionally been late to meetings. So had others, but he was the driver, the focal point, if not the heart of the team. As the face of Sanford Racing Trey also had extraordinary obligations, meetings with sponsors, guest appearances, media interviews. Sometimes there were scheduling snafus, but these days Trey was blamed for every mix-up, and team members seemed to take that as license for them to be sloppy, as well. On one or two occasions he'd vetoed his crew chief's recommendations—to his own detriment—but those things came with the territory. Then he missed a team meeting when weather grounded him on his return flight from Mexico. Internet rumors began spreading about his dead-of-night trips south of the border, and people started questioning his dedication to the sport—and his integrity. The family had made the decision at that point to bring Ethan and Gaby in on the truth, that Trey had epilepsy and the trips to San Meloso were not for a romantic tryst but to see his neurologist. The hope had been the crew chief and PR rep could squelch the scuttlebutt without going into detail. Despite their best efforts, they'd been only partially successful.

NASCAR racing was not an individual sport. It wasn't one person against another. It was one team and their high-performance car against a group of other teams and their high-performance cars. The number of variables was inestimable. Some mistakes could be pinpointed, but they were in the minority. Yet his team seemed to be holding him responsible for all of them.

I'm getting paranoid, he thought. Not a good sign.

On Friday he took sixteenth position in the lineup. Not the pole. Not close to it. At least he was in the forward third of the pack.

He didn't keep it. His first pit stop ran more than fifteen seconds. The second seventeen. Fortunately other teams weren't doing much better getting their acts together. When three cars spun out directly in front of him, he managed by skill and good fortune—he never discounted Lady Luck—to move up before the yellow flag went up.

By the time the white flag waved for the last lap, he was in third place behind Kent Grosso and Zack Matheson. First would have been better, of course.

He called Nicole on her cell phone that evening only to discover she was busy at the hospital and wasn't able to chat. He told her he would see her the next day.

"I need another IV here," he heard her instruct someone. Then she said distractedly into the telephone mouthpiece, "Good. See you then," and hang up. Not exactly the reception he'd hoped for.

"I THOUGHT I HAD IT in with the other Dickens," Nicole muttered, sidestepping around Trey along the middle bookcases and *accidentally* brushing against him in the process. It had happened before. One of his hands would reach out and caress her on a shoulder, a hip, an arm; the warmth of contact would ratchet up her desire for more. "I've been meaning to reorganize these stacks. Dad separated books by age and provenance, rather than by author or title. Granddad found an autographed first edition of *A Tale of Two Cities* in a Morocco market in World War Two. I guess the real miracle is that it arrived home intact."

"Here it is." Trey stretched up to a shelf above Nicole's head and gently slipped the volume from its place.

"How's your shoulder?" Nicole watched him examine the faded cloth cover with the leather corners. He'd extended his right arm to retrieve the book rather than his left, but that was probably because he was right-handed.

"I don't know, Doc. We could go up to your bedroom so you can examine it. Maybe have me do some exercises…to ensure it's properly aligned and functioning."

"It's a tempting offer." Her mind conjured up images of her unbuttoning his shirt, slipping it off his shoulders, her palms stroking the muscular contours of his chest. "Perhaps I should do a preliminary evaluation right here."

"Anything you say, Doc. Just tell me what to do."

He was offering her an opening and she'd be a fool not to accept it. "Put the book down," she directed in a stilted, commanding voice.

"Yes, ma'am." With as much of a straight face as he could muster, he set the precious first edition carefully on the writing table.

"Turn around and face me."

He positioned himself as ordered.

She moved up to within half an inch of him, caught the woodsy scent of aftershave and male. "Place your hands on my hips."

"Yes, ma'am." He instantly obeyed.

"Now, put your arms around me."

He needed no additional instruction. He drew her into his arms in a loose embrace.

"How does that feel?"

He peered down at her, humor and pleasure dancing in his eyes. "It feels wonderful." Did his voice tremble a little, as if he were holding his breath?

"No pain?"

"Does hormonal discomfort count?" He slowly brought his lips to hers as he tightened his encirclement of her. She welcomed him, felt the connection she'd known was there.

"You seem to be functioning very well," she murmured a minute later, still ensconced in his arms.

"Appearances can be deceiving," he reminded her. "Closer examination may be called for. Perhaps a comprehensive anatomical comparison we can conduct more privately."

She laughed. "There's certainly nothing wrong with your imagination. It seems to be working fine."

"Oh, I have a very active imagination, one that begs to be put to good use."

Timing was everything. The phone rang. The look in his eyes reflected her own annoyance. She dropped her hands. "I have to get this. Sorry." Reluctantly she extricated herself from his embrace, stepped to the writing table against the wall and picked up the instrument.

The hospital, of course. One of her patients was showing symptoms of infection. She dictated a series of steps. "And continue the morphine drip." A few seconds later she hung up.

"Serious?" Trey asked. His sincerity in the question didn't surprise her, but it did please her. He had the Sanford reputation; however, she already felt she knew him well enough to know he genuinely cared for people.

"Not yet, but it could become serious if it's not attended to."

"You don't have to go in?"

"I'm staying right here. Now, where were we?"

She watched apprehension visibly flee from his features, but not the other kind of tension that had taken over his body. "You were in the process of conducting a preliminary examination," he said, "to determine if I have fully recovered from the shock to my system when I first met you."

She nearly giggled as she closed the distance between them. Raising her hands, she rested them on his chest as if she were smoothing out his shirt. What she came in contact with, however, were the solid contours of well-developed muscles. Her own pulse chugged into quick time. "Yes, I remember now."

He slipped his arms around her waist.

She arched up against him, looked into his eyes. "I think we had better continue this upstairs."

"You're the doctor," he replied. "I guess that means you're in charge."

"Wise decision." She ducked out of his embrace, scurried to the doorway. "Race you to the second floor," she dared him and was gone.

She was halfway up the stairs when he flew past her. She arrived breathless at the top to find him standing there, arms crossed, peering down at her imperiously. "I race. You doctor. Remember? That was the deal."

"Please don't go too fast for me, Mr. Race Car Driver." This time she did giggle as he picked her up and carried her to the master suite.

CHAPTER EIGHT

"YES, DOCTOR, OF COURSE. Thank you. I'll make the appropriate arrangements. Please give my best to your daughter."

Nicole hung up the phone. Dr. Halsey's daughter was suffering complications from the surgery she'd undergone several weeks earlier, and he wanted to spend time with her. Nicole would fill in for him again at the NASCAR race in Michigan.

Her pulse fluttered at the prospect. How could it not after their afternoon of lovemaking? A few minutes later the doorbell rang and Trey appeared on her front porch, wearing jeans that seemed to have been custom designed for his long muscular legs and a red knit shirt that outlined the equally impressive torso she'd explored so thoroughly. Her heartbeat rose another notch at the recollection. The Sanford cap on his head was slightly askew. They'd spoken last evening after the race at Pocono. He'd come in third. She was proud of him and wished she could have been there with him. That was then. Now…

"Looks like I'll be joining you in Michigan," she told him. "Dr. Halsey called. He notified NASCAR I'll be filling in for him this weekend."

Trey took both her hands, pulled her toward him and touched his lips to hers. "Perfect."

The kiss or the weekend plans? The glow inside her said it didn't make any difference.

"I was about to suggest you and your brother join me this weekend," he said. "You can fly with me and the team Thursday and come back with us on Sunday night."

The invitation was enticing, but Nicole hesitated. "Trey. I'm not sure about Dave. We used to take him to races when he was small, but the excitement was sometimes too much for him and provoked seizures."

Dave flew down the staircase. "That was ages ago, sis." Obviously he had overheard their exchange. "My meds are different now. I've never been to Michigan. It'll be fun."

Nicole shifted her gaze from teenager to driver, unsure of herself. It was true her brother hadn't had any seizures in nearly two years, but she didn't want to provoke one. If he hadn't overheard the invitation, she would simply have declined it and not informed him of the missed opportunity, but she couldn't undo what was already done.

"How about calling Dave's neurologist and checking with him," Trey suggested. "If he says it's okay—"

"Dr. Gaston won't." Dave's tone was bitter. "If he had his way I'd be wrapped in cotton for the rest of my life, eating cold cereal and drinking warm milk. Yuck."

"A slight exaggeration," Nicole protested mildly. "He's just looking out for your welfare."

"I'd rather die of a seizure than of boredom." Dave threw himself into the upholstered chair by the telephone stand next to the staircase.

Trey looked at him and chuckled. "I don't think those are necessarily the only alternatives." He turned to Nicole. "How about it?"

She appreciated Trey's generous offer, but she was more inclined to side with the neurologist. Maybe if Dave's episodes were the absence kind, like Trey's, she wouldn't be as leery, but she'd witnessed too many of her brother's convulsive seizures to dismiss them lightly. Still…

"I'll call Dr. Gaston and see what he says. He may want to adjust your medication—"

"So that I'll be so zoned out I won't even know I'm at the NASCAR race?" Dave intoned angrily. "How about just letting me be me? Or are you ashamed of having me around? Afraid I might have a fit and embarrass you in front of your friends?"

"Dave!" She was shocked. How long had he been harboring this crazy notion? "You know better than that. I've never—"

"Why don't you make the phone call," Trey interceded, "and find out what the neurologist thinks before we make any decisions."

NICOLE WAS PLEASED WHEN Dr. Gaston pronounced her brother fit for the trip to Michigan, but she was worried, too.

"I don't understand," Trey told her when they were having lunch in Charlotte the following day. "You wanted me to open up to your brother so he would know epilepsy doesn't have to limit his horizons. Now he has a chance to do something he wants to do, and you're balking."

"I'm not balking," she insisted. "It's just that…" She sipped her iced tea without finishing the sentence.

"It's just that what, Nicci?"

She raised her head and studied him, remembering the taste and texture of his skin, the sensation of his hands all over her body. He could become addictive.

He blinked slowly and raised an eyebrow, reminding her he was waiting for her to speak, to explain. She had to gather her wits to recall what they'd been talking about.

"My parents owned a small plane. They loved to go flying, mostly on weekends when they had the time. They took me along and we took Dave with us a few times, but he didn't do well. The quick changes in altitude, the g-forces on takeoff and landing, made him sick."

"And provoked seizures?"

She nodded. "The first time Dad thought it might be the newness of the experience, but when it happened again, he decided that it would be best if Dave waited a few years before he went up with them again. Sometimes children outgrow epileptic seizures."

Trey nodded. "I bet Dave was unhappy about being left out."

She lowered her eyes again. "We didn't tell him."

"But he figured it out on his own."

She sighed unhappily. "He has epilepsy. He's not stupid. When he was turning ten and Dad asked him what he wanted for his birthday, Dave told him to go flying with us and be allowed to take the controls."

"And your father said no."

"What he tried to do was not say yes."

"But, as you say, Dave isn't stupid."

She toyed with her tea glass. "He figured that out, too, and got really upset, so upset he had another seizure, which made my father feel even worse."

"How long ago was that?"

"Eight years."

"And Dave hasn't been flying since?"

Nicole set her jaw and took a deep breath. "Two weeks later our parents were killed when their plane crashed."

Trey reached across the table and took her hand. "I'm sorry."

"It was one of those *freak* accidents. That's what every-body said. Dad was a good pilot. So was Mom for that matter, but that day he was at the controls. As best the investigators were able to determine, they got caught in one of those sudden summer storms that seem to pop up out of nowhere and were hit by a downdraft. The plane was slammed into the ground." Her eyes watered and she had to fight to keep her voice level. "They were killed instantly. At least it was quick," she managed to squeak out before her voice failed altogether.

"I'm sorry," Trey said again. "It must have been terrible."

With the gentle tightening of his hand on hers, she felt as though she were being swallowed up by the warmth of his touch. She wanted to crawl into it.

"Dave's seizures got worse after that," she went on, "and became more frequent. They've been under control the last couple of years, thanks to the medication Dr. Gaston has prescribed, but I'm concerned about this trip to Michigan."

"I wish I had known," Trey said. "On the other hand, that was eight years ago. He's not a boy anymore. Obviously his doctor agrees, since he's given the go-ahead."

She pursed her lips. "Not unconditionally. He wants Dave to double one of his medications for the flight and also while he's at the track. He's concerned about the level of external stimulation, the noise, the excitement he's going to be subjected to."

DAVE STRAINED TO ABSORB the world spinning around him. He'd watched NASCAR races on TV hundreds of times, knew the names of the drivers, their crew chiefs, who their sponsors were. He recognized faces, could recall records and statistics. Vibrations crept up his legs, bombarded his chest, whirled around his head. Yet it was all a thousand miles away. The noise drowned out conversation in a sea of conversations. The smells of the track, hot asphalt and scorched rubber, the throbbing of supercharged engines pent with impatient energy were all there in front of him, touching him, yet remote, otherworldly.

Standing in the garage area, he watched Trey talk with his crew chief, interact with his team members, witnessed the camaraderie, the easy rapport underlaid with tension, worry.

It was a facade, he thought. They were not nearly as sure as they pretended to be. Was this the normal state of affairs? Did all teams wear masks of confidence when in fact they were scared about not getting it right?

Dave cheered on Friday when Trey qualified for the third spot in the opening lineup for the Sunday race. He hovered as closely as Ethan Hunt would allow him during the practice runs and the tweaking sessions that followed, listened in on their radio talk. He felt special when, in the garage area amidst discussions that sometimes sounded like arguments, Trey winked at him, reassuring him without a word that he was glad Dave could be there with him. It was confusing. Trey was a lot like his dad, happy to have him there, eager to teach him stuff, except Trey wasn't old enough to be his father. He was more like a friend, like…a brother, someone he could count on, someone who understood where he was coming from.

Saturday evening Dave watched the NASCAR Nationwide Series race along with the rest of the Sanford team. He cheered Shelley Green when she came in third, less than two seconds behind the leader. He ate more pizza in three days than he had in the past month, some of it hot, most of it not.

Cold pizza and stale cola, a smirking team member had remarked, was the breakfast of champions.

He missed Jenny. He wished he could have invited her to come with them, but it would have been presumptuous to even ask on his first time out, and his sister, his CFS, would have freaked. It was bad enough having Nicole hovering over him at every opportunity, always asking him how he was feeling, did he need a rest, was the noise too bad, were the lights causing him any problems, as if he were a little kid who had to be asked repeatedly if he needed to use the potty. He almost told her to bug off, to get off his back, but then he saw Trey and clammed up. Nicole could be a pain in the butt, but Dave knew he'd be in even worse trouble if he came between her and her boyfriend. What Trey saw in her baffled him. She was pretty, he supposed, but not that pretty. It wasn't as if Trey couldn't have any woman he wanted and line up the rest in waiting. Why he'd pick Dave's control freak sister was beyond him.

He watched the race on Sunday from the top of the hauler, from behind the wall of pit road, from the top of Trey's motor home, from the top of Adam Sanford's motor home, on TV, even for a while from the infield care center with Nicole. It was exciting, even with half his brain anesthetized.

From third place, Trey quickly moved up to take the lead. He stayed in front for three laps before being overtaken by Will Branch. The two battled it out for twenty laps, when Jem Nordstrom moved in and dominated the field until Trey had to come in for a pit stop.

Trey rejoined the pack in fourteenth place, moved up to sixth, got slammed against the wall by Finnegan Jarvis but managed to pull out and keep going, losing three positions in the process. He snaked his way again to the lead, held it for another four laps, got tapped by Nils Booker, fell back into eighth place and languished there for another dozen laps.

Dave watched it all, listening intently on headphones to the cool exchanges between his favorite driver, his crew chief and spotter, straining to keep his attention focused on details while the world around him seemed to be mashed into a soupy stew of impressions and blunt-edged stimuli.

Damn the meds. Damn the doctor for prescribing them, and damn his sister for insisting that he take them.

"GOOD JOB, BRO," Adam crowed when Trey climbed out of Car No. 483 in the garage area.

Trey grinned. Fourth place wasn't spectacular, but it was respectable. Now if he could keep the momentum going. Making the Chase for the Sprint Cup was going to be tough, but it was still possible.

Dave was grinning from ear to ear, as well. Trey was glad the kid was able to come with them and that he'd gotten through the event without incident. He knew the meds were making him feel dim-witted. If he got through this trip without having a seizure maybe the next time the dose could be reduced.

The flight home was quiet. Return trips after a race that hadn't brought them to Victory Lane usually were. Trey had the plane stop in Asheville where he'd left his car. He would take Nicole and her brother home, hopefully spend some private time with her, sure Dave would be over at Jenny's house the rest of the evening.

Then Dave threw a monkey wrench into his best-laid plans.

CHAPTER NINE

THEY WERE between Asheville and Brevard. Trey was driving his SUV, Nicole in the passenger seat on the other side of the central console, Dave sprawled out on the backseat.

"You going over to see Jenny tonight?" Trey asked him.

Nicole glanced over, her cheeks slightly hollowed, her lashes hooded, the gleam under them betraying her participation in the conspiracy for them to be alone. Trey had the urge to reach across the console take her hand in his. He wanted to feel her touch, the warmth of her skin against his, but the darn buckets seats made it impossible to do so without being obvious.

"Yeah, soon as we get back," Dave muttered. He seemed preoccupied. Could just be the medication catching up or wearing off, Trey decided. Just as well her house was within walking distance.

"Want me to drop you off there?" Trey asked.

"No. I'll head over after." Not as enthusiastic as Trey would have expected, but they were still a half hour from Brevard, enough time for him to recover his enthusiasm. He'd have plenty to tell his girlfriend.

Trey couldn't help glancing over once again at Nicole. She was facing straight ahead, but he could see from the curve of her mouth that it wasn't the countryside she was contemplating. They'd been playing eye tag for the past three days. The desire and hunger simmering between them was impossible to hide—at least from each other. He wondered how many other people saw it, too, but he didn't let it worry him, except in the sense that he wanted to protect her reputation. Dr. Nicole Foster wasn't another Trey Sanford girlfriend. She was someone special. His Nicci. He didn't want his image to taint hers.

"We'll be there soon," he remarked lightly.

She turned her head toward him, the smile on her lips more than agreement and much more than a smile. A tease. A promise. A challenge.

He pictured them entering the old Victorian house alone, closing the door to the outside world, him taking her in his arms and kissing her deeply, then leading her up the stairs—maybe carrying her again—to her bedroom.

"Better slow down," she said in a murmur.

Slow down? Did she think his patience was endless? Slow down? Maybe the second time.

"Trey?" She sounded concerned this time. He shook his head and looked over at her.

"Our turn." She pointed.

He'd passed it. He applied the brakes hard enough to put pressure on their seat belts, executed a U-turn and negotiated the turn to Brevard when Dave made his announcement.

"I want to get a VNS."

Nicole didn't overreact, but even without seeing or touching her, he felt her stiffen. It took several seconds before she looked over at him, her expression unhappy. Because of her brother's statement or the interruption it represented to their plans. Probably a little of both.

She swiveled in her seat to the extent her shoulder harness allowed. "Dave, I'm not sure that's a good idea."

"I hate feeling like a zombie."

"I know you do, but this was the first time you've been

flying or gone to a NASCAR race in years. You did really well this weekend, so—"

"It was like watching everything underwater," Dave countered. "I hate it."

"Now that we know the medication works," she went on, "maybe Dr. Gaston will cut the dosage for next time. You know this is a matter of trial and error."

They arrived at the house on Grover Lane. Lights, set by electric timers, burned in the central hallway and living room on the left, as did one in a bedroom upstairs. Trey pulled down the single-lane driveway and stopped in front of the two-car garage. He had turned off the engine, and they were about to alight from the SUV when Dave repeated, "To hell with the meds. I want a VNS."

Nicole remained calm, then she slowly peeked over at Trey, a silent plea for help burning in her eyes.

"Did you hear me?" Dave demanded. "I said I want a VNS like Trey's."

Bowing her head, she acknowledged softly, "Yes, I heard you."

Another beat of stress throbbed.

"Let's unload the luggage," Trey suggested, "then we can sit down and talk about this."

Dave leaped out of the vehicle and opened the rear hatch. Trey could feel the tension emanating from the woman sitting on the other side of the console. He wasn't surprised by Dave's request and couldn't imagine Nicole was, either, but the timing sure was lousy.

He reached over and clasped her hand. "Hear him out, Nicci," he said in a low voice.

She nodded, her eyes bright with frustration. "I will. It's just that—"

He raised his hand and stroked her cheek, though he knew touching her was a mistake for both of them.

She opened her mouth to say something, then closed it. The temptation to lean forward and kiss her lips was impossible to resist, but as he started toward her, Dave exploded with, "You guys coming?" and slammed the hatch door.

Simultaneously taking breaths, they gave each other plaintive smiles and stepped out of their sides of the vehicle. He watched her stride to the mansion's back door, then he grabbed the largest suitcase Dave had unloaded and left the other two for the teenager.

The three of them entered the house. Nicole snapped on the light switch.

"I'll take these upstairs." Dave tucked one of the smaller cases he'd brought in under his arm, picked up the larger suitcase and trudged to the central staircase.

"Any ice cream in the freezer?" Trey asked Nicole, though he wasn't hungry, even for ice cream, and doubted she was. Dave, on the other hand, was a teenage male; he'd never turn down food.

Nicole snorted and nodded, letting the shadow of a smile hover on her lips.

Attagirl.

SHE WAS ANGRY, BUT she wasn't exactly sure why or at whom, which exacerbated matters. Every time Trey touched her she plunged out of control, yet she had no reason to be angry with him. He'd done everything she'd asked him to do and more, starting with telling Dave that he had epilepsy and following up with this trip to Michigan. She wanted the best for her brother, but she also had the sense that he was slipping away from her. She could understand some of it, especially his growing desire for independence. Nobody liked to be told what to do, when to do it, how to do it, but that was what parents did, protect their children. She'd become more of a parent to him than a sister since their folks died. Someday she would have to let him go, like all parents, but not yet. Things were still too uncertain.

She didn't miss the irony that while her brother was learning independence from Trey, she was growing more dependent on him. Not legally or morally but emotionally. She craved his company, the joy that possessed her when she was around him.

Inviting Dave to go to Michigan had been generous of him and, thanks to Dr. Gaston's insistence on a stronger dose of his medication, Dave had tolerated the flights without difficulty and the incredible stimulation of three days of NASCAR racing without a hitch.

But this fixation on getting a VNS...

She certainly didn't oppose the concept. She was in favor of anything that might make his life better, but all her research indicated the device wasn't suitable for the tonic-clonic form of epilepsy.

Dave bounded long-legged back into the kitchen. The two men sat quietly at the table in the breakfast area like a couple of kids, while Nicole dished up the ice cream. A huge mound for Dave, a lesser quantity for Trey and a portion barely half of his for herself.

Dave shoveled a soupspoonful into his mouth and swallowed it almost instantly. Brain freeze, Nicole thought, as she took a much more modest teaspoonful from her smaller dish.

"Okay," Dave muttered between bites, "let's talk about me getting a VNS."

"From everything I've read," Nicole said, an eye on Trey, soliciting his help, "VNS technology isn't appropriate for your kind of seizure disorder. Trey has passive absence seizures. They're different from your active and violent kind."

"Tell me something I don't know, sis," Dave muttered. "Trey's VNS keeps him on track—" he gave a lopsided grin at his unintended pun "—without a whole bunch of medication."

"I still take some," Trey reminded him. "A VNS is not a cure, only a treatment. The same treatment doesn't work for everybody."

"They let you drive in NASCAR." He put down his spoon, having demolished his bowl's contents. "Do you have any idea what this weekend was like for me?" He snorted. "No, of course you don't. You've never had to take the drugs Dr. Gaston prescribes."

"They prevent you from having seizures," Nicole contributed.

"So for the one percent of the time I might have a seizure, I have to spend the other ninety-nine in a freakin' trance. Screw it. It isn't worth it. If I can't get a VNS, I'll just cut out the meds and take my chances. At least when I'm not having a fit I'll be able to experience real life, not some stupid fog."

"Whoa—" Trey raised a hand "—hold it right there. Not taking your meds won't improve matters, and you could do real harm to yourself. If they're not working the way they should or the side effects are too strong, tell your doctor—"

"You don't think I have?" Dave shoved his bowl aside, almost knocking it over. "And I've told Nicole, but they don't care."

"Dave—" Nicole begged quietly.

"You just want to control things. You don't give a damn about how it makes me feel."

"Dave," Trey said sharply. The angry young man was about to further elaborate, when Trey bellowed, "Shut up."

The teenager froze and stared wide-eyed at him. So did his sister. A long moment elapsed.

"Take a deep breath," Trey ordered more moderately but

with unmistakable authority. "Just keep your mouth shut for five minutes before you say something you'll regret later." He turned to Nicole. The troubled frown on her face triggered instincts that went back to the dawn of man—to protect the woman he loved.

He loved her? The realization came as a warm shock.

"Let's give Dave a few minutes to calm down," he said in a voice that had her studying him for a moment before she rose unsteadily to her feet.

Trey placed his hand on the small of her back and escorted her out onto the back porch. She was trembling, or was he the one with the shakes? Something was happening he didn't understand, something momentous. The heat of the day had long passed, leaving behind it a soft caress of mountain-perfumed night air. It was the kind of evening when a man alone with a woman would fold her in his arms and kiss her.

He stroked her back. "You okay?"

"Tired, I guess. It's been a long weekend."

He put a smile in his voice. "That's usually a good thing. Most people complain race weekends are too short."

"I should have prepared better for this. I knew eventually he'd ask about getting a VNS." She pressed into his gentle massage, as he'd hoped she would, and said no more. The only sounds between them was the twitter of crickets and the pounding of his heart.

She pivoted around to face him. He lowered his hands to her hips as she nestled against his chest. He kissed her lightly on the lips. When she didn't resist, he plunged deeper and was rewarded by her joining him in an exploration that had his every sense and natural reaction on alert.

Trey could hear water being run in the kitchen behind them.

"We better go inside before he decides to bolt." She

turned toward the doorway, then abruptly stopped on the threshold. "I'm glad you're here with me."

His pulse gave another thump. He was about to assure her he planned to always be there for her, but she'd already gone inside. He wanted to haul her out again and take her in his arms. He stepped through the doorway.

"Why can't I have a VNS?" Dave challenged his sister before Trey even had a chance to close the door behind him.

Nicole resumed her place at the table. Dave had taken her bowl and Trey's to the sink, leaving the table clear. He'd even wiped away the sweat rings they would have left.

"We've been over this before," she answered reasonably. "Trey's absence seizures result from an interruption of the electrical stimulation to the part of the brain that controls neurological impulses. A Vagus Nerve Stimulator fills the gaps and evens the flow of current to the affected part of the brain, thereby maintaining neurological stability. Your seizures are the opposite. Instead of a lack of stimulation, your neurological system produces too much, and you experience convulsions rather than lethargy. In technical terms, it's the difference between hyper and hypo. One is too much, the other is not enough."

"But if a VNS can even out his hypostimulation, why can't it even out my hyperstimulation?"

Trey looked at her with a well-what's-the-answer expression.

"I'm not a neurologist," she admitted. "I'm an orthopedist."

"So you don't really know what you're talking about."

"Dave—" Trey shot him a warning glance "—when you can make the lame walk, you might be in a position to criticize someone else's medical expertise. Until then, I suggest you watch your manners and show respect for those who can do those things."

There was a long beat of silence. "Sorry," Dave finally mumbled, head down.

"May I offer a compromise?" Trey turned to Nicole. "How about contacting Dr. Gaston and confirming with him that a VNS isn't appropriate for Dave's from of epilepsy?"

She nodded gratefully. "I'll call him first thing in the morning."

CHAPTER TEN

TREY HAD A FULL AGENDA of promotional stops on Monday after the team meeting, which took him away rather than toward the mountains. He visited an auto-parts shop, a bookstore and a school and finally drove into Raleigh, where he met with a sponsor headquartered there. He spent the night alone, wishing Nicole were there with him. After their discussion the previous evening, Dave called his girlfriend to tell her he was coming over, only to learn her mom had suffered a relapse, so the two teenagers settled into a long telephone conversation. A few minutes later the hospital called. This time Nicole had to leave. Realizing he wasn't likely to get any private time with her that evening and having a long day ahead of him tomorrow, Trey drove back to Lake Norman.

He called her Monday afternoon, but she was again at the clinic and didn't have time to talk, except to invite him to dinner at the house with her and Dave the following evening.

"Isn't Tuesday your night at the clinic, too?" he asked.

"I traded shifts with Dr. Preston again. I have good news to share with you."

"Were you able to reach Dave's neurologist today?"

"I called, but he and his wife left over the weekend for a Mediterranean cruise and won't be back for a month."

"Sounds nice. Did you talk to anyone else there about a VNS?"

"No. They have a lot of new staff and I didn't want to explain Dave's medical history with someone I didn't know, especially over the phone. Dave has his usual quarterly appointment in five or six weeks. We can discuss it with Gaston then."

"A long wait," Trey remarked, "for an answer that could change your life. Have you told Dave yet?"

"I called him a few hours ago. He wasn't very happy about it."

"I don't imagine he was."

She didn't get it, Trey realized. Maybe intellectually she did, but at the gut level she didn't understand that her brother wanted control of his life, to be able to dive headlong into the surf, not just stand along the shoreline watching other people while the tide undermined the sand around his feet. A plan began to form in his mind, but he needed to do some checking first. Better to wait before saying anything.

He asked what the good news was, but despite his best coaxing, she refused to tell him. Games, he loved them, loved the idea of playing them with her,

He heard the passion in her voice. He felt it, too, and wished he was with her to explore it further.

Tuesday was as hectic as Monday. He drove to Wilmington where he gave a talk to a group of tourists and their kids within sound of the Atlantic lapping at the white sandy shore. His podium faced the wall of windows that afforded a panoramic view of the beach where people played in the sand, snoozed in the sun, splashed in the gentle waves of the vast ocean. His mind kept imagining Nicole in a skimpy bikini running along the shore, stretched languidly on a blanket, her arms outspread, beckoning him.

Twice, as he listened to the surf pound, he passed his right wrist over his chest, over his heart.

It was after seven when he pulled down the driveway to the back of 427 Grover Lane and uncoiled himself from behind the wheel.

By the time he reached the base of the steps, Nicole was standing at the top. Trey's heart raced. He instinctively rubbed his chest. His prayer wasn't *be still my heart,* but *brain, don't let me down now.*

"Sorry I'm so late." He looked up at her smiling face.

"Haven't you heard? The party doesn't start until you get here."

He should have had a quick comeback, something about her stealing his line, but for the life of him, he couldn't think of one. All he wanted to do was to touch her. Vaguely he was aware of the beat of music coming from upstairs.

"You hungry?" she asked.

"Would you be offended if I said I'm not, at least not at the moment? After twelve hours on the road I'd like to stretch my legs for a few minutes. Care to go for a walk?"

In response she quietly descended the steps and linked her arm with his, as if she belonged there. They kissed softly. He inhaled her light flowery scent and felt like…a man coming home. Home. The word had an allure he'd never truly considered before.

"What's your good news?" he asked as they strolled down the driveway hand in hand and turned left onto the road. The street was quiet but for chattering songbirds getting ready to nest for the night.

"NASCAR has offered me a regular contract as an infield care center physician. I'll be attending the races on the East Coast and a few other locations."

She squeezed his hand. "Trey, I'm so excited about being a part of the NASCAR community. I told you my folks had a motor home, that we used to go to races as often as we could—until Dave's epilepsy grew worse." She paused for a moment. "After they died, I took Dave to one race, but it was a disaster."

"His seizures—"

She nodded. "I sold the motor home. Part of me hated to do it—it held so many pleasant memories—but it was time to move on."

"We went through a similar thing when my father died. Of course, our relationship with him was a little more complicated than yours was with your parents."

They arrived at a natural turnaround and started back toward the house.

She looked over at him. "What kind of man was he?"

It wasn't an unusual question. After all these years Wild Bobby seemed to be more remembered for his death in the arms of his latest mistress than his accomplishments on the track, which had been considerable.

"There's no easy answer. He was a complex man, a selfish bastard who could be incredibly generous when the mood struck him. He laughed a lot, but it was probably as much at people as with them. He was smart, yet he could be incredibly stupid. He was married to a woman who loved him, yet he…" They walked on. "He was a man of passions, but I don't think he was capable of love, except maybe for himself."

"Was he a good father?"

Trey snorted. "If you ignore his leadership by example, yes, he was. He was very protective of us. He certainly looked out for me when I was diagnosed with epilepsy. Oh, there was self-interest involved, to be sure. He didn't want to be tagged as the father of an epileptic! As if there were some shame involved, but he had my best interests at heart, too. He was a good teacher as far as my brothers and I were concerned. He liked to show us things, explain how they worked, let us fiddle with them, as long as we didn't hurt ourselves. I think he liked kids." He chuckled softly. "I told you he was a complicated man."

"You loved him, didn't you?"

Trey took a few more steps before answering. "I guess I did."

The house loomed with its inviting wraparound porch and stained-glass windows, its dim, formal library chock-full of aging tomes and deep Persian rugs.

"Have you or Dave ever been to the West Coast?" he asked as they mounted the steps.

She shook her head. "I've been up and down the Eastern Seaboard, but I've never been west of the Mississippi."

"How about you and Dave flying with me and the team out to California for the race this weekend."

Her features brightened, then shadowed. "I have to work—"

"Surely your colleagues will trade shifts with you if you explain why." He folded her hand in his. "The trip to Michigan went without a hitch, Nicci. This is the next step. I bet he'll do fine."

Her indecision encouraged him. She hadn't said no. "Arrange for a few extra days off at the beginning of next week, as well. We'll take my private plane instead of the team plane, so we can go off and do touristy stuff while we're out there, see some of the sights."

"Are you serious?" She gawked at him as if he were crazy, but Trey could hear the note of intrigue with the question. "When do we leave?"

They both turned to see Dave standing at the foot of the steps.

"Dave," Nicole drawled in a sympathetic tone, "I'm not sure—"

"It'll be a long flight," Trey interjected. "If we leave tomorrow afternoon—"

"Tomorrow afternoon?" Nicole exclaimed. "I've got to check my patient appointments, coordinate with my associates—"

Trey suppressed a chuckle. Without even realizing it, she'd agreed to the trip. The hang-up now was the scheduling. "We can stop overnight in St. Louis and go on the next morning. That way the flight won't be so long."

"What about your team? Won't they expect you to go with them when they leave Thursday?"

"I don't always fly with them. Sometimes I have promo stops I have to make."

"Do you this time?"

"Don't worry about my schedule." In fact he would have to make a few last-minute changes that Adam wouldn't be pleased with, but he could arrange to make up for them later. "By the way, do you have passports?"

"Passports? Why would we need passports to go to California?"

"In case we want to cross a border, silly," he said with a lighthearted laugh. "Ever seen Victoria, British Columbia, or Baja California?"

"We got passports last year," Dave announced, "when I thought I might be going to Montreal for a swimming competition. Except my sister here wouldn't let me."

"Because you would have had to fly through New York with two- or three-hour layovers going and coming, and I couldn't arrange reservations on the same flight—"

"As if I needed you," Dave snapped angrily. "I went to Michigan without a problem. Oh, that's right, you were there to hold my hand. I forgot. What would I have done without you?"

He brushed past her into the house and ran up the stairs.

"I don't know what's gotten into him lately," she muttered.

"Did you really not let him go on the trip with his team?" Trey asked.

"He makes it sound so sinister. I discussed it with the swimming coach and we agreed that with the amount of medication he would have had to take for the trip Dave wouldn't be able to swim at his best, and that would have been a problem, not just for him, but for the team."

It sort of made sense, Trey conceded to himself. He wondered, though, if the coach had completely agreed or if he'd caved under Nicole's relentless pressure. If the kid were really that sluggish from his meds, the coach could have left him on the bench.

"Dave would still have been able to cheer his teammates, though."

The warmth that had been in her eyes only minutes before turned cold as she stared at him. "So you disagree with me, too. You think I should have let him go—"

Trey held up his hands. "Sweetheart, I'm not saying you were wrong. If I have the timing right, he'd had his last seizure less than a year before. You were right to be concerned, but I can see how Dave would look at it differently. He saw only limitations. Now, with things under better control, he can focus on broader horizons. Isn't that why you wanted me to tell him about me? Blame this outburst on me—"

Her head shot up. "No." The word was drawn out like a plea. "It's not your fault. If it's anyone's it's mine."

"Ah, Nicci." He put his finger under her chin; she gave him a rueful smile.

"That's better." He touched his lips to hers. As he did, he felt the tension in her body begin to melt. Her arms wound around his waist and she deepened the kiss.

Suddenly she pulled away. "Dave might see—"

Trey grinned and shook his head. "Nicci, honey, I don't

think your brother would be shocked at seeing us kissing. I've been trying to tell you, he's a big boy now…well, not exactly a boy. I think it's a safe bet he not only knows about the birds and the bees, but about the chemistry of physical attraction, maybe even the biology."

She locked her fingers behind his neck. "Well, yes, I suppose."

Trey smothered a chuckle. "Like I'm attracted to you, sweetheart, and based on the way you just kissed me, I suspect the attraction might be mutual."

IN TRUTH NICOLE WAS struggling to decide how she felt about Trey. Oh, the physical attraction between them was real enough. When she was with him, he made her feel special, as if she were the only woman in the world. He was certainly not the kind of man she thought she'd ever be drawn to. Her father, the male role model in her life, had been a sweet, gentle, compassionate man. Dependable, a thinker.

Trey was…Trey was sweet and gentle, too, but he exuded so much energy, so much self-confidence and pure stamina he was almost overpowering. He was fun to be with, unpredictable and exciting. She found herself thinking about him, about being with him more and more, but there was something about him, too, that scared her.

CHAPTER ELEVEN

TREY HAD A MAJOR BATTLE on his hands when he talked to his brother the following morning. As owner of Sanford Racing, Adam wasn't happy about his driver not flying to the coast with the team. He was even more displeased when Trey said he wanted to reschedule an appearance in Greensboro later Wednesday afternoon at an auto-parts store belonging to one of their biggest sponsors.

"You're ticking off a lot of the very people you depend on. You know that?"

"You're blowing this out of proportion," Trey retorted. "I probably don't travel with the team a quarter of the time."

"Because of sponsor commitments. They understand that, but this isn't about a sponsor. It's about your latest girlfriend. Are you trying to emulate Wild Bobby, little brother?"

Trey ground his teeth and was about to snarl a terse two-word epithet and slam down the phone when Adam mumbled, "Sorry. That was unfair."

Until six months ago, when a blogger started speculating about Trey's late-night flying, all of which had been done alone from a quiet, out-of-the-way airstrip near Concord, Trey had had the reputation of being discreet about the women in his life.

"Look," Adam continued in a more conciliatory tone, "I'm not trying to push your buttons. What I am attempting to do is wake you up to the fact that you're...*we're* not doing very well this year on the track or off. I can't say it's solely because of your driving."

"Gee, thanks."

"You're probably as good behind the wheel as ever, but you're not consistent. People understand that. It can even be a positive force to bring them together. They like to root for the underdog. But your unexplained absences and the scuttlebutt about secret trips to Mexico are making people uneasy."

A few of the stories on the blogs were so ludicrous they would have been funny but for the fact that some people, even on his team, wanted to believe them. One rumor held that he had a whole family ensconced in a luxurious hacienda outside Mexico City. Another portrayed his secret family as living in a squalid village in the Mexican hinterland.

Wild Bobby would have laughed his head off.

Except it wasn't a laughing matter, not for Trey.

Other blogs speculated he was sneaking off in the dead of night to buy drugs in Mexico. In a perverse way it was true. Not illegal narcotics, but perfectly legal, prescribed medications for his epilepsy, drugs he didn't want to purchase in the U.S. because he was afraid the information would leak out. A discreet way to purchase them at home could certainly have been arranged in a pinch, but he also needed to visit Dr. Price at the neurological clinic in San Meloso on a regular basis so she could monitor his VNS and make any adjustments to it or his meds. Its proper functioning wasn't for comfort or convenience. At 180 mph it was extremely critical for himself and everybody around him.

Ethan managed to squash the gossip that Trey was using or trading narcotics by insisting that under no circumstances would he work for a driver who abused drugs, and that if he caught anyone spreading that kind of slander, the person would be fired with prejudice, which essentially meant they wouldn't be able to find a job on another team.

The stories of Trey having a mistress or secret family in Mexico persisted, however. Ethan tried to put the kibosh on those rumors, as well, but with less success. Given Sanford history, it seemed perfectly natural for people to jump to the conclusion that the family's current unmarried driver was following in Daddy's footsteps.

Now Trey was actively contributing to his womanizing reputation by flying an attractive young woman and her kid brother to California in his private plane instead of traveling with his team.

"What I'm suggesting," Adam said, taking up where they'd left off, "is that you learn to be discreet. Your love life is your own business. Don't make it anybody else's, and don't tell the people whose livelihoods depend on you that they rank second to your current squeeze. Even Wild Bobby was smarter than that."

THE RACE IN THE Sonoma Valley of northern California was one of two road courses in the NASCAR Sprint Cup series. Just shy of two miles in length, it snaked through twelve turns to both the right and the left, some of them hairpin tight. It also went up hills and down, requiring the driver to shift gears frequently. To further complicate matters, the race was driven clockwise instead of counterclockwise. Set in the middle of magnificent wine country, attendees were as likely to be picnicking on blankets in grassy fields while the cars roared by as sitting in any of the several small, scattered grandstands.

For a stock car driver this course was a unique and compelling challenge.

Trey loved every bit of it—the frequent changes of direction, skidding through flat turns, the constant shifting of gears and the unpredictability of the drivers around him. He swiped his right wrist across his chest more on this track than on any other. The VNS had never let him down. He went into the race with utter confidence it would keep him—and the people around him—safe.

"You have three major competitors out there," Ethan told him the night before the race. Trey had qualified for the number nine position on Friday. "Jem Nordstrom, Finnegan Jarvis and Mitch Volmer. Volmer's never won here, but he's come in second three times and has always finished in the top ten. Jarvis has gone to Victory Lane twice, Nordstrom three times. He's from this part of the country and cut his teeth on road courses. Even when he doesn't win, he inevitably finishes in the top five."

By the fifth lap Trey had moved up two positions.

By the eighteenth he was in third place, behind Haze Clifford and Mitch Volmer. Nordstrom was two cars behind him, driving conservatively, biding his time.

Four laps later, Trey was in the lead. He stayed there for the next six laps, until Volmer overtook him on Turn Eleven, the sharpest on the course. The two continued to play cat and mouse for the next eighteen laps, each taking the lead from the other for nine of them.

By the time Trey came in for his first pit stop, he was leading the pack again.

A four-tire change, a full tank of gas and a slight adjustment to the right rear wedge and he was back on the course in less than fourteen seconds. He passed Nordstrom, who was pulling in for his first pit.

Competition heated up during the second phase. Four cars had crashed and were eliminated when they misjudged Turn Seven, a sharp unbanked right turn. Another driver had to call it quits because of a transmission problem, and a sixth car lost a wheel, slammed into a barrier and totaled his front end.

Most of the other cars were now in it to finish, not to win.

Jarvis, who'd been hanging consistently in the middle of the lead pack, began to move up.

Volmer continued to hold either first or second place.

Nordstrom hung close behind him but—Trey's spotters assured him—not too close.

Another four-tire pit stop and gas up. No adjustments this time.

Trey was feeling good.

"Don't get overconfident," Ethan cautioned him. "Nordstrom hasn't made his move yet, but he will—and soon."

They'd both been in for their last pit stops. The ravages of skidding through sharp turns that had very little, if any, banking made four-tire changes mandatory. Brakes, used in moderation on standard oval courses, were in constant use here and were burning hot. Transmissions, normally left in high gear once on the track, were being slammed constantly as hairpin turns demanded snappy deceleration and acceleration. Engine temperatures, too, were rising.

Five laps to go.

Volmer in the lead, Trey dogging him.

Clem Dawson popped up from nowhere out of Turn Seven and slipped between them. While Trey challenged Dawson, Jarvis snaked through an opening on the right and inched ahead of Trey. Dawson lost it on Turn Ten, which was shallow but still "unnatural" for a stock car driver. He recovered but lost his position.

Volmer, Trey and Jarvis threaded notorious Turn Eleven and were coming up the back side in a straight line, when Nordstrom ramped it up out of the hairpin, took the left, the inside of the track, going into Turn Twelve. At Turn One he pulled ahead of Jarvis. At Turn Two he overtook Trey. He switched sides, swung to the right going into Turn

Three and screamed past him in front of the Turn Three stands.

There were two races now. Between Nordstrom and Volmer for first, Trey and Jarvis for third.

Trey brushed his wrist across his chest, stomped the gas pedal and shot up to Jarvis's right side on the straight-away leading into Turn Seven. On the inside. If he braked too early, Jarvis, with a wider arc to travel, would have the split-second advantage he needed to pull ahead and cut him off. If Trey tapped the brakes too late, he wouldn't make the turn.

Every hundredth of a second counted. They reached the slanted line. Decision time. Jarvis slowed fractionally without touching the middle pedal, was forced nonetheless to go wider still. Trey downshifted, his engine screaming in protest, his tachometer redlining. He skidded through the inside of the right-hand turn. The rear end whipped to the left. He wasn't sure his back tires, billowing blue-white smoke, were ever going to grab.

Jarvis had moved up on the outside, but by then he began to pinwheel. He downshifted but still had to hit his brakes to regain control. That was all Trey needed. He slammed the gas pedal into the floorboard and roared ahead.

He came in third by a car length.

"Great job, little brother," Adam said over the intercom.

"I THOUGHT WE WERE going to Victoria in Canada," Nicole commented the following morning after they had been airborne over an hour. Trey had taken them along the scenic northern California coast to Redwood National Park, cut inland and shown them the vast forests of giant trees. "Why are we turning south?"

"Because that's where Mexico is," he answered lightly. "North of San Francisco, I'll head west, so you can see the bay and the Golden Gate, then we'll head down to Silicon Valley, cut over to Santa Cruz, check out Monterey Bay, follow the coast down to San Diego, and finally head into Mexico. We should be there in time for a late lunch."

"Yummy," Dave piped in. "I love Mexican food."

It was close to one o'clock when Trey set his plane down on a dirt airstrip not far from the Sea of Cortez, which separated mainland Mexico from Baja California.

"Why here?" Nicole unbuckled her seat belt. The landscape beyond the window was not particularly impressive, nor had the small town they'd flown over been.

"This is San Meloso," he explained. "Santa Ysidra Hospital is just on the other side of the hill. It's where Dr. Price has her practice."

Dave caught on before his sister did. "Dr. Price? Isn't she the neurologist who gave you the VNS?"

Trey kept his attention focused on Nicole, though he spoke to the boy. "I've arranged with her for you to receive a full medical exam and evaluation, if that's what you want, to determine if a VNS is appropriate for your form of epilepsy."

Nicole's eyes went wide as she stared at him, then she turned to her brother. "Dave, did you know about this?"

"Well, no, but—"

"Do I have this right?" Nicole said to Trey. "You arranged for a medical evaluation of my brother without talking to me about it, without even telling him?" She put it in the form of a question, but it was more like an accusation.

Realizing he wasn't getting the reaction he'd expected, he tried to salvage the situation by grinning innocently at her. "I figured it would be a nice surprise." He flipped switches. The engine wound down to a sputter and stopped. "Fortunately, Dr. Price was able to squeeze him in at the last minute."

"This is fantastic." Dave clenched his fist in the air.

Nicole still had her eyes riveted on Trey. They weren't soft and loving. "Surprise, huh? It feels more like an ambush."

"Ah, honey," he pleaded, "don't be like that. I expected you to be pleased, especially since you weren't able to reach Dr. Gaston. Dr. Price can do a full medical and neurological workup and determine if a VNS is right for Dave. She can even perform the surgery here, if that's what he wants."

"Hot damn." Dave rushed to the clam door behind the cockpit and pressed the control button on the side that lowered the folding stairs to the ground. Dry heat bellowed into the airplane's cabin. "Come on. Let's go."

"Trey," she said patiently, "I don't object to the tests and evaluation, but you should have talked to me before making any commitments. The treatment he gets is still my responsibility and my decision. Suppose this doesn't work out. If I had been given a chance to consult with Dr. Price privately first, I could have prepared Dave. Frankly, I'm surprised she would even discuss another patient with you." She unbuckled her seat belt but made no move to vacate the seat. "That wasn't very professional on her part."

Trey paused to let a spike of temper subside. "I didn't give her a name. I simply asked if she would be available to run some tests on a friend of mine and evaluate the advisability of a VNS. When we meet her—if we meet her—for all she'll know the friend is you. Assuming, of course, we're still friends."

Nicole didn't crack a smile. "I know you mean well," she said in a tone that simmered just below fury, "and I appreciate what you're trying to do, but you—"

"What's the big deal, sis?" Disturbed by their slowness in vacating the plane Dave had moved back from the open doorway to the cockpit. "I told you I want a VNS. Trey's arranged for me to get one. Why are you being such a control freak? I'm the one with epilepsy, remember? This isn't about you."

"Hold it." Trey swiveled in his seat to face the boy. "First, let's stay civil and not allow emotions to take over. Second, you need to know, Dave, there are no promises, no guarantees. Your sister is right. I should have discussed it with her and you. We don't know what the test results will be. It could turn out that a VNS isn't right for you."

"It will be," Dave insisted, and Trey knew the kid would be heartbroken if it didn't turn out to be true.

CHAPTER TWELVE

SANTA YSIDRA WAS A sprawling two-story complex, a self-contained medical center with its own laboratory, X-ray, CT and MRI facilities, as well as operating rooms and an emergency-care capability. It was located on a parcel of land that also contained several other structures, among which was Dr. Price's personal residence, a dormitory for her medical staff, a dining hall and recreation center, in addition to several communal homes for long-term patient care.

None of the buildings, predominantly stucco or adobe, were new; several looked as if they could do with another coat of whitewash, if not more extensive maintenance. The atmosphere, however, was one of permanence and stability, rather than deterioration.

Trey led them to the main building and the large Saltillo-tiled reception area. Behind a waist-high counter sat a diminutive women with long, shiny, jet-black hair and equally dark eyes, who couldn't have been older than her early twenties.

Trey greeted her in Spanish. She gazed up at him admiringly and said something Nicole didn't comprehend.

"What—" she started.

"Dr. Price is expecting us and wanted to be notified as soon as we arrived," Dave translated.

"Study Spanish in high school?" Trey asked.

Dave nodded. "Had to take two years, but I signed up for two more."

Nicole surveyed the area. The place was hardly impressive. Other than the chairs, a battered twisted-leg table in a corner piled with dog-eared magazines and a box of toys beside it, the room was spartan. The limed walls were uneven and scarred, though the place appeared to be clean.

"Trey!"

In the open doorway next to the counter stood a middle-aged woman with rust-colored hair generously salted with gray pulled back into a disorganized bun at the nape of her neck. She was slim but wide shouldered with large hands. As she came forward, her sharp hazel eyes shifted from one to the other of her visitors.

Trey made the introductions, identifying Nicole as Dr. Foster, an orthopedist.

"Let's go to my office."

Dr. Price led them to a cramped square room. Charts and forms overflowed the corners of a faded oak school desk, from the top of a filing cabinet and a box on the floor beside it. There were only two visitor chairs in the room. Dr. Price rolled her chair out from behind the desk, shoved a stack of papers away from one corner of her desk and perched herself there.

"Now, before we get started," she said, "I suppose you ought to tell me who my patient is."

"I am," Dave announced, probably for the first time in his life sounding proud of it. At her request, he then described his condition and rattled off the list and dosage of the medications he was taking.

Her questions were extensive and thorough. She made no statements or comments that could be perceived as judgmental about the treatment he was receiving, leaving Nicole to wonder if she agreed with Dr. Gaston's assessment.

"VNS implants have been successful in some cases of tonic-clonic seizures," she told her new patient, "unsuccessful in others, so I won't make any promises, and I must warn you not to get your hopes up." She rose to her feet. "But we're getting ahead of ourselves. First, let's run some tests, then we can discuss alternatives, if there are any." She addressed Trey. "I assume you're planning to spend the night."

"Spend the night?" Nicole turned to Trey, but he didn't see in her eyes the same images that were filling his mind, the two of them together alone in each other's arms.

"We need to run an EEG," Dr. Price went on, "which, as you know, is best done over a several-hour period while the patient is sleeping."

"Where will I—"

"At Trey's request," the older woman said, "I've reserved two rooms in our guesthouse. They're not luxurious, but I think you'll be comfortable there. You are welcome to eat in our dining room or you can go into the village, whichever you prefer. Trey will tell you the food around here isn't bad, especially if you like it spicy. Nothing exotic, but wholesome and satisfying."

"We haven't had lunch yet," noted Dave, the perpetually ravenous teenager.

"You must be starving, then. Tell you what. Since you've been fasting, this is a good time for us to draw blood. While we're doing that, Trey can show your sister to the guesthouse. After they've freshened up, they can pick you up here. The three of you can grab a bite in town and look around. You'll have to be back here this evening by eight, no later than nine." With a nod of agreement from the others, she moved to the door. "Come on, kid, let's go stick you with needles."

"IT WAS SO THOUGHTFUL of you to make advance reservations for me," Nicole said as she walked beside Trey along the stone-paved path that led to the guesthouse. His impulse was to take her hand, to swing it between them like a couple of youngsters, but she was still angry with him for bringing them here without consulting her first. He'd obviously screwed up, misjudged.

"Do I detect a note of sarcasm?" Trey asked mildly.

"It's just that these spur-of-the-moment impulses take so much preplanning."

No use exchanging barbs. He wasn't going to win. "What do you think of Dr. Price?"

After a moment's pause, Nicole responded evenly, "The diplomas on her wall are certainly impressive. M.D. from Johns Hopkins, surgical training at the Mayo. Member of half a dozen medical boards and neurological organizations. Outstanding credentials. She seems very nice, too. I'm sure her patients like her."

"You should see her with kids. She's great."

At the foot of the shallow hill, in a grove of cedar trees, they came to the guesthouse, a rambling single-story, hacienda-style building with pale stucco walls and a weathered roof of faded orange Spanish tile.

"Number eight is to the right." He led her in that direction.

"You know your way around."

"I've probably stayed in every room here at least once. Some of them feel almost like home."

"Where is your room?" *So she could come visit?*

He wanted to tell her, *In the suite right next to yours,* that there was a connecting door for their convenience and discretion, but his short-notice request hadn't allowed that. There had been only two openings available, the suite where he usually stayed and a separate single bedroom.

"On the other side of the building." Far, far away.

She tried not to react, but he saw the momentary crease

in her brow. Was the frown in relief or disappointment? At this point he didn't know.

He used the key—no fancy slide cards here, but an actual brass key on a steel ring—opened the heavy oak door, pushed it inward and stepped aside for her to precede him. The room was spacious and comfortable. To the left was a river-rock fireplace with a raised hearth, flanked by two niches. One contained shelves with books and pieces of pottery. The other served as an entertainment center with a flat-screen TV and various electronic components.

"There's an Internet hookup for your laptop," Trey noted.

To the right was a wrought-iron table and four matching chairs, and in the far corner beyond a low wall, a small kitchen. The colorfully tiled counter held a basket of fruit and an old-fashioned black telephone.

"Straight ahead—" Trey waved toward the arch opposite the front door "—is the bedroom and bath."

"This is lovely." Nicole spun around to take it all in.

"Dr. Price has good taste."

For the first time, Nicole smiled. "Except for her own office."

"I don't imagine she spends a whole lot of time there."

Nicole ambled into the bedroom. He followed her, but his attention wasn't on the room, which was as large as the one they'd just left, or the king-size bed that he'd hoped to share with her. He was focused on the woman and her reaction to their surroundings.

"My luggage is already here!" she exclaimed.

That morning he'd suggested they take their things with them—in case they decided to spend the night somewhere else. He knew she'd been picturing Canada. Surprise!

They returned to the living area. "You've thought of everything." She made the statement an accusation rather than a compliment.

He wanted to tell her he was thinking of more than luggage and furniture, but he suspected she knew that, even if she didn't want to acknowledge it to him. He was pretty sure the same ideas were dancing around her mind, too.

"Thank Dr. Price for the hospitality," he said.

"VIP treatment." He still wasn't sure if he could detect her earlier sarcasm in the comment and didn't dare ask.

"I'll give you a few minutes to freshen up and unpack." He glanced at his watch. Nearly three o'clock. "Will fifteen minutes be enough, or would you like more time?"

"Fifteen minutes will be fine."

He was inclined to trudge to his room but refused to give in to his depression…disappointment at the way things were developing. These weren't the emotions he'd antici- pated feeling here today.

Number twelve was not nearly as commodious as the suite he'd just left. The single room might have been part of an outdated motel in a little West Texas town. It contained a double bed and a single nightstand, an alcove hiding a toilet, sink and shower, no tub. There was a bare pipe rack for his clothes—his suitcase was parked under it—and an old tube-type TV perched on the end of a writing table.

Heaving a discontented sigh, he hung up his clothes, washed his hands and trod back to the luxury suite.

ALMOST IN SPITE OF herself, Nicole was impressed. Her accommodations were as tasteful and comfortable as a private residence, even to the little details like a tooth- brush holder in the bathroom. The whirlpool bath was downright luxurious and the separate, oversize shower with its multiple heads was invitingly decadent. Enough room for two, she noted, unbidden.

She frowned. There was something stimulating about decadence.

Trey had done a masterful job of swallowing his emotions at her reaction when they'd landed. Bringing them here may have been the right thing to do—it was—but why couldn't he have been up-front about it?

Because he was afraid she'd say no. Would she have? She wanted the best for her brother, but she also felt an obligation to make sure he didn't get hurt. Dave was utterly confident he would get a VNS and all his problems would be solved, that his epilepsy would be cured. She wished it were that easy. For Trey it seemed to be, but—

A tap on the door made her jump. She knew it was Trey and her body involuntarily responded with a tingle of anticipation. She couldn't remember ever having this reaction to a man before. It heightened her senses, made her more aware of him, of her, of the two of them. Strange, her surroundings seemed to fade into obscurity when she was in his presence, yet she was more aware of herself, of him when she was with him, too.

"Ready?" He was silhouetted against the bright afternoon light. Tall, stalwart and so damn male. She had to remind herself she was angry with him, then had to ask herself why.

"The rooms all right?" he asked as they trudged up to the medical complex.

"Fine, fine. Thank you."

They mounted the last few broad stone steps, their hands swinging at their sides within inches of each other. She waited for him to reach out, hoped he would. When he didn't, she asked, "Yours okay?" When he didn't answer, she said, "Your room?"

"Oh, yeah, fine."

Great. Now he was angry with her for being angry with him.

Dave was pacing restlessly in the reception area when

they arrived. His face brightened into a wide smile on their appearance, with the kind of enthusiasm she hadn't seen in his eyes in a long time. *Don't get your hopes up,* she wanted to warn him and oddly felt her resentment at Trey spike. Dave was going to be turned down, his hopes of escape from the curse of his disorder shattered. Trey would go on to race stock cars, and she would be left to deal with her brother's resentment and depression.

Dr. Price came out to join them. "I know you're all hungry, but if you can hold off a few more minutes, I'd like to show you around, Dr. Foster."

"Nicole, please. And I'd love to see your facilities."

"I'm Denise."

The complex was a warren of interconnected buildings. The treatment rooms were brightly lit and sparkled with state-of-the-art technology and equipment. No costs had been spared, no corners cut.

As a neurologist, Denise's main interest was seizure disorders. "Progress is slow," she pointed out. "There are so many roads that seem to lead nowhere. Along the way, though, we often find solutions to problems we're not looking at. The medication for restless leg syndrome, for example, was and still is prescribed for symptoms of Parkinson's disease."

"Ahem," Trey muttered some time later. "I hate to interrupt this medical confab, but if Dave and I don't get caloric supplementation pretty soon, Dr. Price—"

"What is it with men?" Nicole asked rhetorically. "They always want to eat."

"You'll have to admit us for malnutrition," Trey finished.

DENISE MADE A CAR available to Trey. He would have preferred Nicole sitting in the front seat beside him, but cramming long-legged Dave into the backseat was impractical, so he took up the bucket seat, while his sister stretched out crosswise behind them.

It was too late in the afternoon for lunch and too early for dinner. Trey took them to a fruit stand near the docks where they purchased fresh guava, papaya and mango, then he took them on a tour of the local area.

San Meloso was principally a fishing village, a classic enclave of small Spanish-tiled adobe houses bathed in the warm sun beneath a perfectly clear blue sky. Nicole, Trey noticed, was looking everywhere but at him, while her brother rambled on about Dr. Price, the tests she was running and his certainty that tomorrow she would insist he receive a VNS immediately.

Trey began to appreciate Nicole's position. If this turned out to be a mistake, if Dave wasn't a good candidate for a VNS, the kid's disenchantment could be a serious problem. On the other hand, Trey assured himself, Dave was young and resilient. He'd be frustrated, but he would go on. Besides, even if a VNS wasn't the answer, maybe Dr. Price could recommend another treatment that would make life better for the guy.

They ate fresh-caught fish at a restaurant within sight of the docks. The place wasn't fancy—this was not a common tourist stop—but the food was excellent.

They arrived back at the hospital a few minutes before nine o'clock. Dave didn't want to admit it, but he was bushed. He'd been on an adrenaline high all day. Trey doubted the kid would have any trouble falling asleep, even if he did have wires and tubes attached to him.

Trey walked Nicole back to her suite, what he had hoped would be *their* suite. She'd mellowed during the afternoon and evening. They'd even laughed, but to his chagrin she hadn't warmed up. She was still upset with him for blindsiding her, and he knew she was justifiably worried about her brother.

When they reached her door, he waited for her to invite him in. She didn't.

"Aren't you going to offer me a nightcap?"

She twisted her key in the lock, swung the door in and palmed the key ring. "No."

He had started to raise his hands, preparatory to folding her into his arms for a kiss. Her curt answer stopped him.

She stepped through the doorway but didn't turn around to face him. "Thank you for dinner. I'll see you in the morning," she mumbled over her shoulder.

Before he could respond, she closed the door. He stood there, staring at the aged wood grain. He wanted desperately to knock on the door and tell her he'd forgotten to give her a good-night kiss.

The ugly truth, however, was that he'd screwed up and deserved the comeuppance.

He did an about-face and retreated to his celibate cell.

CHAPTER THIRTEEN

THE SUN WAS JUST PINKING the eastern sky when Nicole turned on the coffeemaker in her suite. She showered and came back to find more than she could possibly drink by herself. She was tempted to call Trey and invite him over to share it with her. The refrigerator was stocked with eggs and chorizo. The pantry had corn tortillas and a variety of salsas, red and green, all the ingredients for huevos rancheros. She resisted the temptation. But instead of feeling triumphant about her self-discipline, she felt defeated. She poured a third cup of the strong, dark-roasted brew but on the second sip realized she'd be wired on caffeine if she drank it. She really ought to put something more solid in her stomach. She was considering the food available and was again enticed by the prospect of Trey sitting across from her when the phone rang.

If she'd had a cup in her hand at that moment, she would have dropped it.

"Did I wake you?" Trey asked from the other end.

The sound of his voice with its hint of playfulness instantly dispelled her annoyance with him. "I've been up for over an hour."

"I thought you might be. I just received a call from Dave. They've completed the tests and Dr. Price is ready to announce her verdict."

"He called you?" Why hadn't her brother called her? *Because Trey is the good guy, and I'm the equivalent of the evil stepmother.*

"I'm on my way up the hill. If you're ready, I'll stop by and we can make the trek together."

She closed her eyes, willing the phone to disappear and him to be instantly there, holding her in his strong arms. "I'm ready."

When she opened the door to him a minute later she wondered how long he'd been awake. He certainly didn't have sleep in his eyes, and the spring in his step was that of a man on an adventure. How much of the upbeat attitude was an act? Was he as apprehensive as she was?

After she closed the door and jiggled it to make sure it was locked, he took her hand. "Still mad at me?"

"I'm not mad at you," she mumbled, aware of the warmth of his hand in the cool morning air, of his broad shoulders above hers, of every part of him and how she wanted to touch and be touched.

"But you were."

"I was annoyed." She wasn't being completely truthful. *Annoyance* was too mild a word. He'd exposed a gulf between them. They might be able to bridge it for the time being, but that wouldn't make it go away. Disappointment? That was closer to the truth.

"And you still are because Dave called me instead of you." His sensitivity surprised her.

"I just hope everything works out." For Dave. For them she wasn't as optimistic.

They arrived at the hospital entrance and, instead of opening the door for her, Trey pulled her around to face him. "I do, too, Nicci." He kissed her sweetly on the lips. "Everything."

Her mind was spinning, her body much too warm, as

they walked side by side down the hall to Dr. Price's office. If he understood what was happening between them and was willing to adjust, perhaps there was hope for them after all.

Trey chose to stand behind Nicole in the office, rather than inconvenience the neurologist in her own space. Nicole glanced over at her brother. He was fidgeting in his seat like a kid on Christmas morning, waiting to open the big present that had the tag with his name on it. He seemed so vulnerably confident he was about to receive the new bicycle he wanted. Suppose he got coal in his stocking? How would he handle that outcome to this adventure? How would she?

Denise stepped into the room, greeted them cheerily and took her seat.

"We can go into the medical details later, but I don't want to keep you in suspense. You want the bottom line. Is Dave a good candidate for a VNS? The answer is yes."

"Yes!" Dave punched his fist into the air.

The vise that had been gripping Nicole's chest loosened and tears came to her eyes. Denise addressed her next comments to Dr. Foster, professional to colleague.

"We ran the usual battery of blood tests, did a CT scan and administered both an EKG and an overnight EEG. We evaluated the variety and dosage of drugs being currently prescribed to ensure they're at therapeutic levels. They are. I'll be glad to show you clinical results of our analysis."

"So when can I get the implant?" Dave asked.

Dr. Price smiled at him. "We can do it today, if you haven't eaten anything and it's what you and your sister want."

"Of course I want it today. Right now."

"Dave—" Nicole's laugh was a release of pent-up anxieties "—slow down a minute. Let's make sure we understand exactly what's involved."

"What's to understand?" he challenged her, obviously on the verge of losing his temper. Was she going to snatch away his shiny new bicycle?

"Take a deep breath, buddy," Trey advised from behind him. "Your sister is right. Let's hear the facts first."

"Tell us about the surgery," Nicole requested.

Denise nodded. "It's quite simple really, similar to implanting a pacemaker. We make an incision just below the left collarbone, insert a device that's about the size and shape of an old silver dollar. A second incision is then made in the neck above the collarbone, adjacent to the vagus nerve. A hair-thin electrical lead is threaded up from the VNS and twisted around the vagus nerve. The entire procedure takes less than two hours and is performed under general anesthetic. You're welcome to observe, of course, Nicole. While there is some initial discomfort following the procedure, it's relatively painless."

"Let's do it." Dave was about to catapult out of his seat when Nicole asked, "What about costs?"

As a professional courtesy Denise might lower or even eliminate the fee for her services and the usual charges for use of the operating room, but there were other expenses she could not absorb except at a loss, such as the cost of the VNS itself. High-tech medical devices didn't come cheap, even at professional discounts.

Denise started to respond.

"I've got the expenses covered," Trey announced quietly.

"What?" Nicole spun around and stared at him.

"I'll take care of the expenses."

Nicole closed her eyes. He was doing it again, barging into an area where he had no right. Did he think she was going to haggle over the bill? She turned back to Denise. "What about the drugs he's currently taking?"

"I'll adjust his medication while he's here and establish a timetable for further dosage reductions."

"Yes! Yes! Yes!" Dave shouted.

Denise smiled. "If there are any adverse effects, I need to be notified immediately."

She sat back and regarded Nicole, Dave and Trey in turn, then continued. "I'd also like to see Dave back here for a checkup in four weeks, and if everything proceeds smoothly, another six weeks later. From there on quarterly checkups will be sufficient. They don't have to be done here. Your regular neurologist, if he's agreeable, can monitor him and make any further adjustments that might be called for."

"That's a lot of traveling for him," Nicole remarked.

"If it's all right with you," Trey said, "he can come with me. I have to be here periodically to be checked out and pick up my meds."

"What about the college team swimming tryouts in two weeks?" she asked her brother. "Will you be able to swim at your best if you're still sore from the surgery?"

"I'll be healed by then," Dave argued back. "I want this, sis."

And Nicole wanted him to have it, but...

"Why don't I leave you to discuss this among your-selves." Denise rose from her seat. "It's a big decision. There's no hurry. Take your time." She squeezed between Dave's chair and her desk, nodded thanks to Trey, who opened the door for her, and then she left the room.

NICOLE GAZED AT TREY. He had no trouble discerning that her earlier annoyance had turned to something more akin to hostility. This trip was definitely not working out the way he'd anticipated, the way he'd hoped.

What exactly had he expected? To be seen as some kind of hero? He supposed it at least looked that way. All he'd really wanted was to help Dave and ease Nicole's burden as a surrogate parent.

His father had been that way, playing one party off against another, twisting things so that in the end he came out looking like the good guy, the reasonable arbiter, when all along he'd been pulling puppet strings, making people do what he wanted them to do because they thought they wanted to do it.

He remembered Adam's cutting remark. *Are you trying to emulate wild Bobby?* God help him.

"Maybe you should put this off until after your tryouts," he told Dave.

Dave stared at him with glassy eyes, like a kid who'd just had his Christmas present taken away. "You, too?"

"No," Nicole said before Trey had a chance to respond.

Dave looked up, his expression skeptical, as though he wasn't sure what he'd heard. "No what, sis?"

"This seems to be an opportunity you can't turn down." She looked at Trey. "Would you see where Denise is and ask her to come in?"

AT TEN O'CLOCK THAT morning, Dave was wheeled into the operating room, anesthetized and received a VNS implant. Nicole observed. Afterward she declined Trey's offer to take her to dinner, choosing to have a tray sent over from the dining hall to Dave's room so she could keep him company. Trey visited, then left to spend the evening alone.

Two days later, he flew them back to North Carolina. Dave was sore but upbeat. His medications had been reduced by nearly half, largely because his physician sister was in a position to observe any adverse reaction he might experience.

As for Nicole, she was polite, even thoughtful, but something had snapped between them, and Trey wasn't sure the loose ends could be connected again.

CHAPTER FOURTEEN

THE RACE THE FOLLOWING weekend was in New Hampshire. The Loudon track was a regular oval with good banking on the turns, but because it was merely a mile long it offered drivers a constant challenge.

"Thanks for joining us," Adam said Thursday afternoon when Trey finally showed up. Dave's surgery had delayed his return from Mexico by a day, necessitating the cancellation of three promotional appearances, a pubic relations nightmare his team-owning brother had not appreciated. "I hope this isn't too inconvenient for you."

"Norbert sends his regards." Trey was referring to the owner of an automotive dealership where he had stopped to make a scheduled guest appearance on the way.

"How's Dave?"

Trey hadn't expected the question. Adam had expressed no interest in the kid till now. "Doing fine. He's still psyched about his VNS, seems to regard the surgical soreness as a badge of honor."

"And his sister?"

That question did surprise him. Adam had tolerated Trey's other relationships with a kind of benevolent amusement—until the rumors started spreading about his "secret" family in Mexico. At that point everybody seemed to regard Trey Sanford's love life as the diversion that was destroying the Sanford team. His older brother, who was currently in a relationship with Tara Dalton, one of Nicole's best friends, could be a cynic, but he knew the Mexican affair was bogus, and he was also smart enough to realize for once Trey had met a woman who meant something to him.

"Monitoring him closely. How's the car?"

"Thanks for asking." So much for their moment of fraternal compassion. "Ethan's concerned about engine performance. They pulled it for maintenance, then put it on the dyno. It showed a couple of minor anomalies, nothing serious at this point, but they haven't been able to duplicate them."

Dynamometers were high-tech test machines that evaluated engine performance and measured horsepower. A flaw that couldn't be duplicated couldn't be fixed and became a wild card no driver or team wanted to have to worry about.

"What about the backup?" Trey asked.

"That's what Ethan wants to discuss with you, whether to start with the backup and hold the primary in reserve."

The decision would have to be made before qualifying the next day. One car could be substituted for the other between qualification and the race itself, but doing so relegated it to the back of the pack of forty-three, regardless of where the primary had qualified.

There appeared to be nothing wrong with Car No. 483 that afternoon when Trey ran his practice laps. The engine growled and howled like a caged lion, roared through the turns and sprinted like a wildcat on the straightaways. Never a sputter or a burp.

"Let's go with the primary," Trey advised Ethan.

He took a discouraging thirty-first place in the startup.

"Drivers have won from the back of the lineup," Ethan reminded him. "Concentrate on where you want to be, rather than where you start. The big challenge is going to be Nordstrom. In taking the pole he also set a new qualifying lap record. He'll fight like hell to stay in front. Focus on moving up in the second pack in the first half of the race, then into the lead pack in the second. By the last twenty-five laps you want to be among the first ten."

Trey nodded. It was a tried-and-true strategy. In every race, the main opponent was the guy right in front of you. He would leave the long-term strategy to Ethan. That's what crew chiefs were for.

As for Nicole, to say she treated him coolly while they'd been in Mexico would be an understatement. She didn't get mad; she didn't argue or raise her voice to him; she didn't even talk down to him. She was painfully polite and invariably considerate, but she rejected every entreaty he made to bridge the gap between them. She declined his meal invitations, his invitation to the race in New Hampshire, even his suggestion that he help her finish cataloging the books in her library she was planning to donate to the local college.

On Friday night he called the house to see how she was doing and to check up on Dave. She wasn't home, her brother told him. Trey wasn't sure if it was the relief from the heavy medication or the continuing euphoria of having his very own VNS that had the kid nearly hyper.

"The world isn't moving in slow motion anymore," Dave told him, not for the first time. Trey marveled that the guy had achieved so much in school and in sports, tethered by so many drugs. "Thanks for getting me a VNS."

"Don't thank me," Trey replied. "Thank Dr. Price and your sister."

"Dr. Price was great. You can probably get Nicole on her cell."

Trey was disappointed that Dave didn't appreciate what his sister had done for him, but a sermon on the phone wouldn't help matters. There'd be other opportunities to play big brother.

"I'll try her cell, then," he said, but he didn't. As much as he wanted to hear her voice, he decided giving her space at this point was probably what she needed.

He called the house Saturday night, as well. He didn't expect Dave to be home and he wasn't, but apparently neither was Nicole or she wasn't answering the phone— to him. The answering machine picked up. Was she there and not answering? He could have left a message, but he wanted a person-to-person discussion, not a person-to-machine semblance of communication.

He started to dial her cell-phone number, then stopped. She probably knew he'd been trying to reach her. She certainly knew where he was and how to reach him—if she wanted to. He may have handled the trip to San Meloso poorly, even insensitively, but he hadn't done anything wrong, and he didn't deserve to be treated with such disdain.

As his brother kept reminding him, he had one job: to win the race tomorrow.

On Sunday he fell back from his starting thirty-first position to thirty-fifth within the first ten laps.

"What's going on?" Adam asked over the radio.

Just then Trey threaded his way into an opening between two cars and shot ahead of them. "Everything's fine."

The first pit stop went well. Under fourteen seconds.

Trey continued to move up. By the second pit stop he had advanced to the lead pack and was in eighteenth position.

The third pit stop was sloppy. Sixteen seconds. They'd analyze it later.

Two laps out of the third pit stop, his engine sputtered. Not a big bang, more a hesitation. Probably no more than a tenth of a second's delay, but the momentary loss of power cost him a chance to move ahead of Haze Clifford.

He called it in. Could be any of several things. Contaminated fuel was one and seemed to automatically shoot to the top of the list, but it could be an electrical problem, a clogged filter, a stuck valve. His father would know, Trey mused. Wild Bobby had an instinct for troubleshooting. For him not every sputter, belch, burp or fart was the same. In that split-second delay he would have zeroed in on the source of the problem. Others could do it, too. Brent had been better than average, but Bobby had been the best.

Four laps later it happened again.

"Electrical," he called in. "I don't think it's fuel. Electrical."

Nothing happened for the next six laps. By then Trey had moved into ninth place. He was beginning to pull around Finnegan Jarvis on the outside after completing Turn Two, when the engine died.

He swallowed the expletives that came to his lips, clamped his hands tighter on the wheel and tried to ease to the right, but it was too late. Mitch Volmer, who had been drafting him, slammed into the left side of his rear bumper, sending him into a spin. Volmer was able to escape, but the car behind him, driven by a rookie named Buck Lazare, didn't. Three more cars were involved in the accident before they all came to a smoke-enshrouded halt on the grass infield.

"You okay?" Ethan asked over the radio.

Trey swiped his right wrist over the VNS buried in his chest. "Yeah, I'm fine. Absolutely fine."

NICOLE MADE A NOTE on the chart for the patient she'd just examined and put it in her out-box for Jeanette to file later.

Time to check on the patient in curtain three, a four-year-old who'd been brought in with a hairline fracture of the left ulna, the result of a fall in a playground. The boy was in otherwise excellent health. At that age the injury would heal quickly and since there had been no actual break, he would probably experience no future problems.

As she walked down the corridor from her office, she heard voices in the waiting room, Jeanette's and another one that sounded familiar. *What was* he *doing here?*

For a moment she couldn't breathe. She couldn't move or think straight. A shiver of longing lurched through her, an ache so profound her knees threatened to buckle. Steeling herself, she stepped into the large waiting room, which was crowded with adults and children. Everyone seemed to be focused on the man who was doing some sort of pantomime. From the cut and condition of the guy's clothes, she would never have recognized him.

"What are you—"

"Meet our new volunteer," Jeanette practically cooed, as she came up beside Nicole.

"Who—"

"Name's Carter Brooks. Started tonight, says he can come in only one or two nights a week and then probably for no more than an hour or two, but he's willing to do whatever has to be done while he's here. From the way he has everyone entertained, I wish it was more often. Sure brightens up the place. Will you look at those kids' faces?"

But the children's open expressions of wonder were in Nicole's peripheral vision. Her attention was riveted on Trey Sanford. She knew there was only one reason he was here—to torment her—and dammit, he was succeeding. He shot her a quick grin and the starch in her spine wilted.

"Did you say Carter Brooks?" she murmured. "Where's he from?"

"The paper he filled out says Hendersonville. I don't recognize the address, but then they're building so many new houses there I can't keep up."

I can't, either, Nicole thought. *Every time I think I have him pegged he surprises me.* "Carter Brooks," she repeated, as if she were trying the name on for size. Where did he come up with that moniker?

He had his back to her as he did an imitation of a tight-rope walker. He reached a bank of chairs across the room, did a snappy about-face, caught Nicole's glance again, winked, then continued his mime, this time swaying as if he were about to fall. He was on a perfectly flat, even floor, yet everyone seemed to be holding their breath, terrified he would lose his balance and fall.

"Be careful," a little girl called out.

Good advice, Nicole mused, but how was one to be careful with a man who was impetuous and impulsive and incredibly generous, with a man whose kisses made her want more? Her mind might advise her to walk away, but her heart was saying, *Come fly with me.*

Carter waved as he wobbled, in appreciation of the girl's tip. Crossing the floor, following the seam of vinyl tiles, he peered up from beneath knitted eyebrows, the twitch of a grin pulling at the corners of his mouth. This time his eye contact with Nicole was brief, but it was more than a glance. It made a connection. She couldn't help it. She smiled.

He reached his destination, an arbitrary spot two tiles from the opposite row of chairs, did a hop, as though he were jumping onto a platform, held up his hands in triumph and turned around to the enthusiastic applause of his audience. He threw kisses, one aimed directly at her.

"Isn't he great?" Jeanette remarked.

Nicole could feel the kiss on her lips, feel his arms around her. "He looks sort of familiar," she managed to squeak out as she watched him take bow after bow in every direction. The ham!

Jeanette chuckled. "I thought the same thing, then I realized he looks a little like Trey Sanford, you know, the NASCAR driver."

Nicole studied him. "Hmm. You think so?"

"Honey," Jeanette replied, "I watch NASCAR all the time, and I know what the drivers look like, especially the hunky ones. Well, this guy isn't as good-looking as Trey Sanford, but he'll do. Come on, I'll introduce you."

Nicole smiled. You ought to see him with his shirt off, with that broad, nicely muscled chest exposed.

"Carter," Jeanette called out. He spun around. She waved him over.

He took one more bow, this one exaggeratedly elaborate, rolling hand over hand as he bent deeply from the waist, then came over to the corner where the two women were standing.

"Carter," Jeanette said, "this is Dr. Foster."

"I've been very impressed with your performance." Nicole tried hard to keep a straight face. "I'm glad you didn't fall off that tightrope. You might have broken something...or dislocated your shoulder."

"It's nice to meet you, Doc. If I dislocated anything, I'm sure you'd be able to put it in its place."

Nicole swallowed. "I'd certainly try. Welcome to our clinic."

"He's going to be a wonderful addition," Jeanette chirped. She was gazing up at him with a come-hither smile Nicole had never seen on the fifty-year-old grandmother before.

"Has anyone ever told you, you look like...what's his name—" She glanced over at Jeanette.

"Trey Sanford."

"That I look like him?" He put a subtle emphasis on *like*. Jeanette didn't seem to notice. "No, not that I can recall."

"Oh, but you do," the other woman gushed. "Just like him."

"Well, gee," Carter demurred, "does that make him lucky—or me?"

Nicole laughed, harder than was probably appropriate under the circumstances. She couldn't help it. Okay, the guy had an ego, but he also had a sense of humor.

"What are you going to do for your next trick?" she asked. "A disappearing act?"

"Oh, I hope not," Jeanette said seriously.

"How about you, Doc? Do you want me to disappear?"

"Stick around," Nicole replied breezily. "You're good for laughs."

"I think she likes me," he muttered behind his hand to Jeanette as Nicole walked away.

CHAPTER FIFTEEN

TREY WAS AN ENIGMA. He was a NASCAR driver, flew his own plane and owned a luxury motor home. Yet he was willing to take a couple of hours a week out of his cramped schedule, go under a phony name and do the most menial jobs other volunteers did their best to avoid, and he did them without prompting or complaint. He cleaned up unpleasant messes, swept floors, stacked supplies and greeted visitors as if they were close family members. He had a knack for discreetly inquiring into their maladies, sympathizing with their difficulties and leaving them with upbeat attitudes. This race car driver, who could be so controlling when he thought he was in charge, was also capable of being incredibly supportive when comfort and encouragement were all he had to offer.

Everybody loved him. Nicole was beginning to realize she did, too.

TREY WAS SWIPING A wet mop across the floor when Dave appeared at the end of the hallway, a pretty girl holding his hand and clinging shyly to his side. She barely came up to his shoulder. Jenny, no doubt.

"Carter?" Dave called out with a chuckle.

Trey came forward.

Dave's grin widened. "I couldn't believe it when I

talked to sis a little while ago and she told me you were working here as Carter something."

"Carter Brooks." He extended his hand to the young lady who was slender but not skinny. Her long brown hair was pulled back in a ponytail with a velvety green ribbon that perfectly complimented her pale hazel eyes. "You must be Jenny."

"Pleased to meet you." She looked around uncomfortably. "I've never been here before. It's so busy."

"Where's Nicole?" Dave asked.

"She was called away to help with an emergency. You need to see her about something?"

"Actually, I came to see you." Dave looked over his shoulder. "Is there someplace we can talk? In private."

"Sure," Trey said. "Let's go to my office."

Dave slanted him a suspicious expression, put his arm protectively around Jenny and nodded.

Trey led them down the hall to the janitor's closet, a big windowless space crammed with mops, buckets and cleaning supplies.

"What's up?" Trey asked, once the door was closed.

"My birthday is coming soon," Dave announced. "I'll be eighteen."

"Congratulations."

"Thanks. I start college in the fall, and I need to be able to drive. Now that I have a VNS, there's no reason I can't."

"True, especially with your medication decreased so much."

"I want you to teach me," Dave declared, then hastened to add, "if you want to, of course. I mean, I know you're busy and you don't have a lot of time, but—"

"Why don't you sign up for a course at a driving school?"

He squirmed. "Because I'm not eighteen yet, so I'd still need my CFS to sign the papers."

"I'll be glad to discuss the subject with her," Trey said. "I'm sure she won't have any objection to your driving now."

"You are, but I'm not. She always has an excuse why I can't do stuff. Besides, I'm tired of asking her permission for everything." He took an angry breath. Jenny squeezed his forearm. "If you don't want to do it or you don't have time, that's okay. I understand." He started to move away. "I just thought I'd ask."

"Hey, you giving up that easily?" Trey objected. "I haven't said no yet."

Dave spun around, his face lit up. "You mean you will? When can we start? Tomorrow?"

Trey laughed. "I'll pick you up at your house tomorrow morning at eight."

"Um, could you pick me up at Jenny's house instead? That way—"

"You won't have to explain to your CFS. Gotcha."

Trey watched Dave and his girlfriend go through the double doors at the end of the corridor. He'd incensed Nicole when he took Dave to see Dr. Price without first consulting her. He wasn't about to make that mistake again.

Two hours later Trey found her in the small lunchroom, sitting at a corner table with a guy in a white doctor's coat. He strolled over. She looked up.

"Dr. Foster?"

She was forced to acknowledge him. "Yes, Carter?"

Being a gentleman, her companion rose. "You must be Carter Brooks." He extended his hand. "I'm John Preston. I've been hearing a good deal about you."

He was tall, not quite as tall as Dave, but he still had an inch or two on Trey, and he was wide shouldered. "From Dr. Foster?" He took the man's large hand.

"No, from Jeanette actually. She seems to think you walk on water."

"Only when the floor is wet."

Nicole remained sitting, observing both men. "Dr. Preston is a pediatrician on staff here," she informed Trey.

He didn't like the way she looked at *Dr. Preston*. Was there something going on between them?

"Pleased to meet you, Doctor." Trey returned the man's firm grip. The guy was too good-looking, not pretty-boy but ruggedly handsome, dammit. Trey wasn't the jealous type, but then he'd never wanted a woman the way he wanted Nicole.

"Is there something you wanted to see me about?" she asked, after tearing her eyes away from the big lug.

"I just wanted to let you know your brother stopped by. I thought you were still in the E.R."

"What was he doing here? Is something wrong? He didn't have—"

"He's fine. He asked me to give him driving lessons so he could get his license before school starts. I said I would. I hope you don't mind." He was rambling, saying too much, trying to justify himself. Preston had already resumed his seat, leaving Trey standing there like a supplicant.

Her eyes narrowed and for a moment there was a familiar flash of annoyance. "He didn't say anything to me. I have no objection. Wow, getting driving lessons from a—" She started to say *NASCAR driver* but caught herself and said, "I understand your schedule is very busy. Will you have time?"

"I'll find it. See you later, Doc." As he turned to go he heard Preston ask, "Why would your brother want driving lessons from a janitor?"

Trey snickered to himself but didn't hang around to hear the answer.

CHAPTER SIXTEEN

SINCE DAVE'S BIRTHDAY was the Thursday before the Daytona race and NASCAR teams deployed for the tracks on Thursdays, Nicole decided to postpone her brother's party until the following Monday, so Trey and any of the other team members who wanted to could attend. Dave's musical friends showed up with their instruments, turning the occasion into a minor bluegrass jamboree.

Except for Jenny and the musicians who had met Trey when he had stopped at the music shop, none of Dave's friends had met him. Nicole suspected a few of them thought Dave might have exaggerated his familiarity with the famous NASCAR driver. Naturally Trey Sanford became an instant celebrity at the party.

Once again Nicole was intrigued by him. He could easily have sucked up the limelight, become the center of attention, but he spurned it. He greeted everyone politely, accepted their commiserations for Saturday night's DNF but then quickly focused the conversation on Dave. Adam and Tara Dalton arrived after the music had begun. Tara's NASCAR book, *Scandals and Secrets,* was due out in the late fall. Becky Peters showed up, as well. She'd dated Trey for a while, but that had been months ago, and it was clear their romantic involvement was amicably broken. She was currently seeing Jake McMasters, who was conducting a private investigation for the Grossos into the disappearance and supposed recent reappearances of Kent Grosso's twin sister, Gina. Unfortunately Jake hadn't been able to get away to accompany Becky.

Nicole and Trey had spoken very little since his arrival at the clinic. She had her duties. He took up his. They passed each other in the halls and nodded greetings like strangers instead of one-time lovers. True, she seemed to find an inordinate number of reasons to march down whatever corridor he happened to be in, and she couldn't help hearing his voice when he was reciting a nursery rhyme to a child there for treatment, but he made no attempt to see her privately. She'd been expecting him to ask her out to dinner or invite himself to the house on some pretext or other, but he did neither. Why not? The only reason he was there at all perpetrating this charade as Carter Brooks was because of her. So why didn't he make a move?

Even when he wasn't there she sensed his presence, imagined him entertaining kids in the lobby, swiping a mop across a hallway floor, talking to an elderly patient or sticking his head inside her door to notify her she was needed somewhere else. In her mind's eye she also saw him ogling her, with a teasing grin, when no one was looking, and the thought alone brought back a longing that hurt like desperation, a need that left her feeling frail and vulnerable. Dammit, he had gotten under her skin again, and that awareness made her angry. He was handsome, that was all, like plenty of other men. And he had a sense of humor that was cute and self-effacing. Generous, too, but that didn't make him a saint. He was a Sanford, after all, and they had a history. He had a reputation, even if the story about his Mexican connection was all wrong. He wasn't right for her. Plain and simple.

She had to smile, though, at the recollection of him standing over her table in the lunchroom shaking hands with John Preston. Two men measuring each other without trying to show it. Trey had obviously been jealous. She'd seen it in his posture, in the way he slanted his jaw when he looked up at the tall physician. What fun!

Today he'd offered her a conspiratorial smile every time he passed her on his way to the buffet table or caught her eye from across the yard while he was talking with someone else. Her pulse went up a notch at each encounter. Could people see the effect he was having on her? Was she making a fool of herself?

Self-conscious, feeling taunted and unwilling to admit—except to her secret self—that she enjoyed the sensation of knowing his eyes were following her, she checked the buffet table again. Of course it needed replenishing. This would be the third time she'd loaded down the platters with cold cuts of meat and cheese, but half the guests were teenage males who could eat their weight in sandwiches, then ask for dessert.

Stepping into the kitchen, carrying an empty tray, she caught a glimpse of Dave's back over by the butler's pantry. She was about to ask him to give her a hand when she realized he wasn't alone. Quietly she drew closer. Her kid brother was involved in a kiss with his girlfriend that would have earned at least an R rating. Without intending to, she knocked the tray against the corner of the butcherblock island. It sang out like a cymbal.

Jenny pulled away, peeked like a frightened deer around Dave's shoulder, let out a muted gasp and bolted for the door, eyes averted from Nicole. Dave stared at his sister from the doorway of the pantry.

"Sorry," Nicole said to him. "I didn't know you were in here. I came in to get more…"

Dave started to follow his girlfriend, his mouth tight with anger.

Nicole suddenly realized the kiss she'd witnessed hadn't been the fumbling experiment of a teenager.

"Dave—" she wanted to come across as reasonable, nonjudgmental "—Jenny's a nice girl. I don't know how far the two of you have gone." She sounded like a grandmother. "I hope you're being responsible and using protection."

Embarrassed and outraged, he glared at her with eyes so sharp they were painful to look at. "It's none of your damn business. So just go—"

His angry eyes shifted to someone behind her and Dave's words froze on his lips. He shot past her, out the door after Jenny. Nicole rotated around to observe his departure. That's when she saw Trey standing in the doorway. Her heart gave a little leap. He was wearing faded jeans and a dark T-shirt that clung to his upper body just enough to set her imagination on a rampage of desire.

"Ah, the hero of our time," she observed. "I suppose I should thank you for saving me from a diatribe."

He met her eyes with a twinkle of his own. "This probably wasn't the best time to bring up the subject of safe sex."

"When is? Or are you suggesting it's already too late?" She picked up the fallen platter.

Trey chuckled softly. "You do realize he's not a little boy anymore—" he leaned against the counter, his hand on its edge, his all-man posture irresistible; she wished he'd extend his arms to her "—don't you?"

Accepting the warmth of his embrace would be so natural. She'd missed him. His masculine scent and the tenderness of his touch made her mind go fuzzy. She had to strain to keep her mind on what they were talking about. "Of course I do," she murmured. "I wouldn't have mentioned the subject if I didn't." She stepped back. Everything was so confusing. Trey. Dave. Herself. "It's... They caught me by surprise. He's been full of surprises since you showed up."

"You invited me here, as I recall. I haven't regretted it. Have you?" He didn't give her a chance to respond. "Better get used to it, Nicci. He's old enough now to go off to college by himself, to drive a car, to do all kinds of adult things. If you want him to act like an adult, you'll have to respect and treat him as one."

"Thank you, Dr. Phil." She turned away. Uncertain. What was happening to her?

Suddenly he was stroking her back. Heat radiated from his touch. It would be so easy to let him fold her into his arms, to wallow in the sensations of his body pressed against hers. She wanted him to tear her clothes off; she wanted to tear his clothes off, feel his flesh make contact with hers. The prospect of being possessed by this man had her melting inside. The realization that he had the power to make her lose control intrigued and terrified her. Again she forced herself to pull away.

"If Dave walks in—"

He laughed. At the situation or at her? Anger again arose. "What's so funny?"

"Us. If your backyard weren't full of people right now, if it were just the two of us, alone—"

He knew what she was feeling. She'd never felt so connected with another person before. To have him in her mind scared her and yet she couldn't seem to stop herself from drowning in the ocean of temptations he provoked.

"But the backyard is full of people, Trey," she said, sounding harsh even to her own ears, "including my brother, so we're not alone." She resumed the task at hand, refilling the platter. "I'd better get more food out there before the horde gets restless."

The corners of his mouth curled up. He had gotten

under her skin, he knew it and was enjoying it. She should be mad as hell at his smugness, and part of her probably was, but another part felt strangely calm, almost content, as if he were a soul mate.

They worked in silence as a team for the next few minutes, replenishing the cold cuts and restocking a large basket with a variety of rolls. Nicole glanced out the open door. Dave and Jenny had returned to the band, which had finished playing "Fast Travelin'" and were striking up "Old Joe Clark." One young couple was twirling around the perimeter of the group, a few others swaying in place to the upbeat music; everyone else was toe-tapping in the midst of conversations. It was impossible not to.

Fifteen minutes later Wayne Rodney, Dave's best friend, a gangly towhead with a broad country drawl, announced it was time to give the birthday boy his presents, or as he put it, *what he had coming.* The first few gifts were of the gag variety: a set of water wings with NASCAR decals on them, ditto an oversize beach ball. A few were more serious: a snorkel for scuba diving and a host of downloads for his MP3 player.

When it was Jenny's turn, she gave him a bracelet, similar to Trey's, that effectively disguised the VNS magnet he wore on his right wrist. That he had an electronic device implanted in his chest was no secret. He had no reason to hide his seizure disorder, especially now that he had "the cure."

At last everyone turned to Nicole. She had been standing on the sidelines next to Trey, laughing and applauding the gifts like everyone else. She wondered if anyone noticed his hand occasionally creeping up her back. She should tell him to keep his hands to himself— at least in public—but she didn't want to make a scene. At least that's what she told herself. Besides, it felt good.

From the base of the tree where they were standing, she picked up a canvas bag and carried it to the center of the gathering.

"This is a big day," she said. "My kid brother isn't a kid anymore, but he'll always be my brother. Still, it's going to be tough giving up my role as CFS."

She stood there, jaw angled, waiting during the extended moment of stunned silence. Then Jenny giggled. Nicole grinned, and the crowd burst into laughter. Wayne Rodney, who was almost as tall as Dave, gave him a slap on the back that had him stumbling forward.

"I considered giving him chain cutters," Nicole went on, "as a symbol of our broken bonds, but the truth is I don't want those bonds to ever be broken. Besides, I found something that might be more fun—sheet music I ran across in the Rags and Riches shop in Brevard."

She dipped into the bag again, this time extracting several sheets of yellowed papers encased in clear vinyl envelopes. "This was printed locally about eighty years ago. I did a little research. The composer seems to have been local, too. I'll let y'all decide if it's worth adding to your repertoire, but I figured it would make a good collector's item."

Dave stepped forward and accepted the gift, glanced at the faded notation. From the expression on his face it was clear he was hearing the music in his head. He reached the bottom of the page, stopped, looked up at the assembly and over at his sister again before announcing, "This is neat." He gave Nicole a peck on the cheek, then concentrated on the sheet music in his hands. "I don't think I ever heard this one before." He started to move toward where the instruments had been parked to try the new tunes out.

"Hang on. I have something else for you." Nicole plunged her hand into the tote once more, this time extracting three large, leather-bound volumes. "These are Dad's journals. I thought you might like them."

"Wow!" Dave's eyes lit up. "This is really cool."

"I don't know if you'll find anything of real value in them, but I figure they'll be interesting to read through."

This time, when her brother thanked her it was with a hug and a genuine kiss of affection. "Thanks, sis. This really means a lot."

The assembly was about to scatter again when Trey stepped up and announced there was another present to be given. "Well, actually two.

"This one isn't very original. A lot of families give them to their kids when they graduate from high school and go off to college. I know I'm not family, but...well, I hope you like it."

He removed something from his pocket and pressed a button. A horn began blaring intermittently from in front of the house. Everyone hurried down the driveway, where they found a brand-new cherry-red Mustang convertible, its top down, parked at the curb. One of Trey's team members had dropped it off when no one was paying any attention.

"Happy birthday, Dave."

"For me? You're kidding." Dave's eyes were wide, his jaw dropped. He virtually tiptoed toward the vehicle, as if he were afraid it would disappear if he scared it. "Is this really for me?"

Trey chuckled. "I wouldn't joke about a thing like a car, buddy. Yes, it's yours."

Dave ran to the curb, Jenny holding his hand all the way, trailed by a chattering retinue of partyers.

Nicole followed, walking more sedately beside Trey, her hands clasped in front of her. He looked over. "You all right? You look a little shaky."

"You're full of surprises, aren't you?" The comment

was made slowly, quietly, and Trey realized there wasn't a trace of humor or pleasure in it.

Trey stopped well behind the crowd that had surrounded the shiny car. "You're upset."

She said nothing.

"You don't approve?"

"I would at least have liked to have been informed, maybe even conferred with about it."

FRUSTRATION RILED HIM. Instinctively he swiped his right wrist across his chest. If she noticed, she didn't show it. What did this woman want? Did every surprise represent a threat to her? Would he have to send her a notice that he would be giving her a Christmas present? Maybe even e-mail her beforehand to say he would be sending her the notice? This was crazy.

"Nicci, I don't understand you. I thought you'd be happy for Dave." But this was Dave's CFS. "Do you not like the car, the make, the model, the fact that it's a convertible or that it's red? Any of those things can be changed."

"After the fact. It would have been nice to have had some input."

Discouragement was escalating to anger. He could handle anger, he told himself. It was pleasing this woman that he couldn't seem to manage.

"What is the real issue here?" Trey asked. "Why do you get so mad when something good happens to your brother?"

"I'm not mad."

He snorted. "Good imitation, then." He tried to put his arm around her, to melt the ice that seemed to have encased her. Should he say he was sorry? For what? Would an apology make any difference? They moved down the slight incline to the curb. Dave had already slipped into the driver's seat, one hand stroking the steering wheel.

"You said there were two presents," Wayne reminded Trey.

Trey studied Nicole. For the guests she was putting on a positive front, examining the spinner wheels and the custom racing stripe, but he could feel the anger simmering behind the plastered smile. Had he not already mentioned the two-part present, he would have held the second half back for the time being, but it was too late now.

"The second part of your birthday present," Trey announced, "is an open reservation at the Charlotte track for the Sanford Experience, a chance to take the wheel of a race car on the track. I'll give you the packet with the information when we get back up to the house. Let them know when you're available, and they'll set it up."

"Wow!" Dave was all grins. "Drive a real race car? Will you be with me?"

"Probably not," Trey replied. "We have people specially trained to guide you through the process. Right now my schedule of appearances is booked solid." To make up for some of the appointments he'd missed by taking him and his sister to San Meloso."

Nicole chuckled. "Just be careful, brother. I understand it's a statistical fact that red cars get stopped more often for speeding and other traffic violations than cars of any other color. Something about cops seeing red!" She offered Trey a saccharine smile.

CHAPTER SEVENTEEN

DAVE STARTED THE ENGINE, overgunned it, fastened his seat belt, turned on his left-turn signal—though there was no traffic on the residential street—carefully checked the rearview mirror and pulled away from the curb. Jenny was seated beside him, her hands folded primly in her lap, an irresistible grin on her face. There was no squealing of tires, no violent swerving out onto the crown of the road, just a calm, cautious departure and acceleration down the quiet, tree-lined street.

Nicole watched him disappear around the bend before turning back to the house. Within minutes the other guests departed, too. Except Trey. Everybody had stopped to shake his hand, as well as hers, before leaving, as if they were a couple.

"I'll help you clean up," he offered, climbing the raised lawn beside her.

"Thanks, but that won't be necessary." Nicole was too aware of his presence, a half step behind her on her left, watching her. She wished he would leave and feared that he might. Nothing would be accomplished by him staying. Nothing positive. "Oh, all right," she conceded. "You can stack the chairs."

She strode among the tables, gathering up the last remaining soiled paper plates, tossing them into the large plastic-lined trash can. Trey started folding chairs.

"Thank you for your help today and your generosity with Dave. You're spoiling him." She tried to speak the words lightly, but she didn't suppose they disguised her sarcastic bite.

"He's a good kid. We all deserve a leg up once in a while." Trey continued to set folded chairs on the metal dolly that would be removed by the rental company later that day. "As for spoiling him, I'll call it that only if he abuses what he receives. Somehow I don't think he will."

He carried another half-dozen chairs to the storage frame. Nicole had finished stripping the tables and was rolling the cloths into a big bundle for the laundry service to pick up.

"As I said," she went on, "I appreciate what you've done for him—and for me."

"Do I hear a *but* coming?" He pushed the dolly off to the side to get it out of the way. "What's really bothering you?"

"I think we ought to cool it for a while," she said casually. "That's all."

"Cool it?" He folded his arms. "What does that mean?"

"I think we should stop seeing each other—"

"Funny, it seems to me the problem, if there is one, is that we don't see enough of each other. I've hardly talked to you since Mexico. I've missed that." When she went on gathering things and didn't reply, he added, "You're going to the race this weekend, aren't you?"

"Yes, but—"

"What do I do if I dislocate my shoulder again? Tell the medics I'm not allowed to see Dr. Foster? That'll sound a bit odd, don't you think?"

"You're trying to make a joke out of this," she snarled. "I'm being serious."

"Joke?" He stopped and scowled directly at her. "You

think I regard breaking up with you as amusing? Is that how you see me, see us? As some kind of joke?"

She didn't seem to know how to reply, or perhaps she didn't want to form the words.

"Trey," she finally murmured, "I don't want to see you anymore."

"I think you've made that pretty clear." He swiped his wrist across his chest and leaned against the rack of folded chairs. "Why? Because I bought your brother a car? Because I gave him the Sanford Experience?"

"They're symptoms of the problem."

"Which is?"

She heaved an impatient sigh. "You don't respect me. You don't trust me as a physician—"

The declaration stunned him.

"Of course I do. You reset my shoulder and I've never had a lick of trouble with it. You're a damn good orthopedist. I've seen you at work on far more complicated cases, too. I've never questioned your competency, not once, and I never will."

"Except when it comes to Dave's disorder."

"So that's it. You think you're supposed to be omniscient." He closed his eyes and prayed for guidance on how he could convince her he didn't want a goddess, but the flesh-and-blood woman she was, with feelings he wanted to touch as a man.

"Nicci, I'm a stock car race driver, and I know a fair amount about auto mechanics, but don't ask me to tune up your SUV. I'll be the first to tell you I can't do it. It's not my area of expertise. Sure, I know the principles that make it run, probably better than the ordinary Joe—or Josie. When the guys at the garage explain what problems they've encountered and detail how they'll fix it, I understand well enough what they're talking about, but that's not the same as being able to diagnose the situation on my own or making the actual repairs."

She was listening. That was what mattered, he told himself. She hadn't completely tuned him out.

"You're an orthopedist," he continued. "You can set bones and repair joints, even replace them with whole new parts. You're a miracle worker, as far as I'm concerned. You fill me with awe and longing."

She lowered her eyes, seemingly embarrassed by his praise. He meant every word of it.

"At the same time," he noted in a lighter vein, "you're not the person I would go to for cataract surgery."

This time, reluctantly, she gave him a thin smile.

"Just as I know *about* mechanics," he went on, "you know *about* neurology. When Dr. Price explained what the VNS could do and how, I have no doubt you understood every medical and technical term, including the details of the implanting and programming process, but because you didn't realize the potential for a VNS in Dave's case doesn't make you a bad doctor. It merely confirms you're not a neurologist, like you're not an ophthalmologist and I'm not a mechanic or an engine builder."

"I should have known."

"Why?" he snapped impatiently.

"Because he's my brother. I should have made it my business to know everything about his condition and all the available options for treatments."

"I get it now. Because your brother has epilepsy you should have become a neurologist, even though your interests and skills are in orthopedics, and if he had a vision problem you should have become an ophthalmologist. If he had a hearing problem you should have been an otologist."

"Stop," she erupted. "You're making a mockery of—"

He bulled on as if he hadn't been interrupted. "Isn't there a medical tradition or ethical standard or some rule somewhere that prohibits doctors from treating their own family members, except in emergency situations? This certainly wasn't an emergency situation, Nicci. It's—"

She tried to object again, but once more he cut her off. "And it is precisely because he is family, your closest family member, the person for whom you've sacrificed so much, that you want to make sure he doesn't have unreasonable expectations."

"I should have looked into VNS technology deeper."

"You have a neurologist whose job it is to do that. If anyone failed Dave, it was Dr. Gaston." And I have failed you, he added mentally, because I don't know how to please you. The thought of not seeing her again scared the hell out of him.

She looked away, and for a fleeting minute Trey wondered if Gaston might have suggested a VNS at some point and she'd rejected the idea. Or had Nicole been the one who had brought the subject up and been discouraged from pursuing it because Gaston wasn't familiar or comfortable with the technology or didn't like being second-guessed?

"Dave thinks I don't want him to have the VNS," she said. "He thinks I never wanted him to."

Trey shook his head. "That's not true, Nicci. He loves you very much, more than you realize. You'll have to forgive him for being a bit stupid right now. He's emotionally tied in knots with everything that's going on, and us guy types don't do real well dealing with emotions, especially when…in case you haven't noticed, he's feeling his oats, if you'll pardon the cliché."

He knew he shouldn't say what he was about to, but it had to be said. "You have a blind spot when it comes to your little brother. It's understandable. You've been more

of a parent to him than a sister. You've given him everything he's needed, gone far beyond what's normally
expected of one sibling for another, but his needs are
changing, sweetheart. He's growing up."

She frowned. Trey wasn't sure if it was because she
didn't like being reminded of the little boy she'd nurtured
slipping away or concern over her changing role in his life.

"Maybe I can help you put this in perspective," Trey
said. "Remember what it felt like to be eighteen, to be on
the brink of adulthood, to be aware of yourself for the first
time as an independent person, full of yourself, eager to
show the world you were a force to be reckoned with?"

"No," she snapped, "I don't. When I was eighteen I
was busy studying for premed, working to earn a scholarship."

He wasn't sure he believed her. "Didn't you have a boyfriend, someone you were madly in love with, even if it
was only puppy love?"

"I didn't have time for distractions."

Oh, you poor thing. But he was smart enough not to say
it out loud. She hurried over to the second buffet table, the
one with the nearly empty punch bowl and the few remaining squares of birthday cake, and began frantically rolling
the tablecloth out from under them. He found the idea that
she didn't want to admit she'd had a crush on some dude
in high school strangely consoling.

"Well, then," he did say, "I guess it is hard for you to appreciate what your brother is going through. Trust me, Nicci,
it's tough for a male to concentrate, to keep his priorities
straight, to tell the difference between wants and needs, when
he's fighting certain instinctive urges." Like the one he was
fighting right now to wrap his arms around her and drag her
upstairs to the four-poster on the second floor…or the couch
in the living room…or the soft verdant grass under their feet.

"He wants, sweetheart," Trey went on, "not just pleasure. He needs his independence."

For a moment she froze, then scrutinized him over her shoulder. "He also needs guidance, not indulgence."

He withstood her penetrating stare and suddenly realized their conversation had taken a wrong turn. "But Dave isn't the real issue, is he?"

She tilted the large glass bowl while she coaxed the cloth out from under it. "No," she stated quietly, "This is not about Dave. It's about us."

He moved over to the stone bench at the edge of the garden and sat facing her. "What's wrong with us?"

She paused, as if trying to make up her mind. "You really don't get it, do you?" She hung her head, then shook it before looking up. "Well, I think the fact that you don't defines the situation as well as anything I can say."

"Does that mean you can't explain it to me or that you won't?"

SHE STUDIED HIS FACE, considered the flash of anger she saw in his eyes and the note of pain she heard in his voice. Much of what he'd said was true. She appreciated the clarity with which he expressed himself, but it also hurt her to realize he'd seen things she hadn't.

As for her blind spot regarding Dave himself, maybe there were times when she was overprotective, too demanding and even controlling, but as Trey had pointed out, her brother wasn't thinking with his brain right now. Someone had to.

About remembering what it was like to be eighteen…she did remember. Too well. Joel had been handsome, a terrific athlete with the broad shoulders, sinewy torso and narrow hips of a cross-country runner. He'd swept her off her feet and into his bed, and he'd made her feel…well…

She wasn't going to go there. She was determined not to make the same mistake again. She wanted more from a man than…fun.

She glanced over at Trey, closed her eyes and willed her body to stop acting like a teenager.

"You're probably right about me being overprotective with Dave," she acknowledged, "like you were right about letting him fly and attend a NASCAR race, about him getting a VNS. You were incredibly generous to take us to California and Mexico, to pay for the surgery in San Meloso and buy him a brand-new car."

He watched her, and she could see the thoughts running through his mind. "You think I resent your being right all the time. You're wrong." She sat on the other end of the stone bench. Several feet separated them, so there was no immediate danger of him reaching over and touching her. She wasn't sure she could survive his touch right now. "What I resent, Trey, is your presumptuousness, your assuming the right to make decisions all by yourself without even discussing them with the people involved. Let me repeat, they were the right decisions. That's not the point."

"What is?"

She closed her eyes for a moment and opened them again. "I don't want to be the recipient of your beneficence, Trey, I don't want your largesse, because someday I'll also be its dupe."

"Nicci—"

"Let me finish. You spoke of independence. I'd like to be respected as a free agent, a thinking, reasoning, quali-fied individual capable of making my own decisions."

"I love you," he said quietly.

She fell silent. Except for her father, no man had ever said that to her. *I love you.* She was afraid she loved Trey, too, afraid that if she gave in to that love she'd become like his mother, a victim, the pitied wronged woman. Trey was manipulative and controlling, which was ironic since that was exactly what he and Dave accused her of being.

"I believe you," she heard herself say. "I believe you think you love me, and I… What I feel for you…it isn't love, Trey. It's…attraction. It's gratitude, but it's not love. I'm afraid of what you'll do to me."

"Afraid?" He was clearly shocked by the statement. "I would never hurt you. You must know that. Never. I love you too much to hurt you or to allow anyone or anything to hurt you."

She almost cried, but she held back the tears. "I hear what you say, but your actions don't match your words. You don't respect me. I don't want a protector, Trey. I don't want someone making decisions for me behind my back, boxing me in, giving me no alternative, no choice in the matter. I don't want to be patronized and patted on the head. I want a *partner* in life."

"Nicci…"

"Please go, Trey. Just go."

CHAPTER EIGHTEEN

DAVE HAD HIS STEREO blasting louder than he would have if Nicole were home, but she'd left yesterday for the NASCAR race in Chicago. This time, unlike the Michigan trip, she practically insisted he go along so she could monitor his progress with the VNS. He'd been tempted. He loved attending NASCAR races, but she also wanted him to stay with her at the infield care center, and that wouldn't have been any fun. Besides, he had things to do at home, the most important one being to take the Sanford Experience.

His CFS had balked, of course, which was one reason he didn't want to do it when she was around. He didn't need a hovering nanny taking the fun out of driving a race car.

"It's too much stimulation, especially when we don't know how well the VNS will function."

"We'll never find out if I don't do things, sis. How about this?" Dave offered. "I'll take Jenny and Wayne with me. They know what the score is. If I'm having any problems, they know what to do and who to notify to get help."

Nicole wasn't happy with the compromise, but she didn't have any convincing arguments against it, either. To placate her they did sit down and review the procedures if he had a seizure. Both Jenny and Wayne had witnessed

Dave having epileptic seizures and had helped him through the convulsive stage. They understood that, contrary to popular belief, it was anatomically impossible for a person to swallow their own tongue, but a victim could bite it, or it could fall to the back of the throat and block the airway.

"Call me before and after you—"

"Sis, I'm going to be fine, but okay, okay, I promise to call you before and after the ride."

She'd deployed for Chicago on Thursday morning and called home that night. Dave assured her everything was fine. The Sanford Experience was scheduled to start at ten the following morning and would last about three hours.

He was suited up, spent over an hour in orientation and training, another half hour on the track with a driver, getting the feel of the car, of the track itself, the banking in the curves, the ruts in the pavement that inevitably developed when forty-three cars ran thousands of laps on it at high speed. Then came full-open laps with the driver behind the wheel.

Finally that magic moment arrived when Dave and the driver traded places. Dave would have liked it to be Trey beside him, but once he got his hands on the steering wheel, who the other guy was didn't matter.

There was no speedometer, only a tach, and no gas gauge, though there was little danger of running out of fuel in this situation.

"That was about one hundred miles per hour," the driver, KL, said through the headset after they'd completed one lap.

Dave put more pressure on the gas pedal, surprised at how stiff it was—not the soft touch of his Mustang.

KL sat quietly beside him. "One-twenty, one-thirty, one-forty, one-fifty."

It wasn't the speed that scared Dave. It was the excitement. His heart was pounding like a jackhammer. He'd been concerned that his incision might hurt but he felt no discomfort, only the thrill that started at the seat of his pants and rippled through his whole body.

"You're doing great," KL assured him.

Dave applied more pressure on the gas pedal.

"One fifty-five, one-sixty, one sixty-five. Check out the turns from different attitudes."

Dave hit Turns One and Two from the bottom of the arc, Turns Three and Four from the middle, Turns One and Two again, this time from the top of the bank.

When Dave finally pulled into pit road he had a smile on his face he wasn't sure would ever come off. He was also surprised to find his hands were glued to the wheel and that, when he managed to tear them loose, they were shaking.

"Awesome," he muttered, then shouted. "Absolutely awesome," he repeated and punched the air. "Man, that was awesome."

He repeated the word a few more times when he got around to calling his sister later.

Dave took Jenny, Wayne and Wayne's girlfriend, Trina, for a late lunch at their favorite pizza place in Charlotte, then they drove home to Brevard in the Mustang. No doubt about it, there was something special about winding along those narrow mountain roads in your own shiny new red convertible with your girlfriend in the seat next to you, making you feel like a million bucks. It was late afternoon by the time he dropped Wayne and Trina off, then he took Jenny home before heading to his house and up to his room.

Now he was alone with his music and his father's journals. He had to admit it had been cool of his sister to give them to him. Their folks had been gone eight years.

Sometimes it seemed like only yesterday that their plane crashed; at other times he wasn't sure he could clearly picture them.

His mom had laughed a lot, he remembered that, and she had been forever fluttering around, doing things. Dad had been fun to be with, too. Dave could remember his mother starting to object to something outrageous he'd said, then she'd stop, cluck her tongue and exclaim, "Oh, you," and laugh, like she'd finally gotten the joke.

Dave missed them.

He thumbed through his father's cloth-and-leather-bound journals. Most of the entries were replete with medical terms he didn't understand, which were flat-out boring. He paged through for more interesting stuff.

Nicole's first pair of Rollerblades, for example, and how she refused to go skating without her knee pads and helmet. Dave chuckled. Even at the age of six she'd been a compulsive little pain!

From time to time William Foster also referred to current events. He mentioned, for instance, the kidnapping of Gina Grosso, the twin sister of NASCAR driver Kent Grosso.

Dave knew the story. It had been written up in all the papers and discussed on the TV talk shows over the past few months. Dean Grosso, who retired as a driver from the NASCAR Sprint Cup Series last fall, had been in the NASCAR Nationwide Series racing at Nashville at the time of his son's birth. He and his wife, Patsy, hadn't been expecting twins, so when Gina was born a few minutes after Kent, it was a complete surprise. Both infants were healthy, the young parents ecstatic. Patsy's parents came to visit; a couple of days later, while Dean and his in-laws were at the race track, Gina disappeared from the hospital nursery.

The local police conducted the initial investigation, then called in the FBI. Dozens of people were questioned, but the authorities got nowhere. Shortly after that an international police task force broke up a baby-selling ring south of the border. Apparently healthy infants and young children were bought or kidnapped and sold to people willing to pay exorbitant adoption fees.

Based on the confession of a woman who worked in this "orphanage" in Mexico, an infant girl, matching perfectly the description of Gina Grosso, had either died of natural causes or been murdered shortly before the police raid took place and the body disposed of. No physical trace of baby Gina was ever found, but the authorities concluded and convinced Dean and Patsy that their daughter was dead.

The kidnapping and death of a newborn infant was a tragically sad story, but it didn't end there. Recently there had been rumors on the Internet that Gina hadn't died at all, that she was alive and well and currently involved with NASCAR in some way. Since the infant's body had never been recovered and the FBI admitted they had no objective proof that the child was deceased, many people thought the story was true.

To Dave and many other people the whole idea seemed preposterous, a cruel hoax invented to stir up trouble. But why? No demands had been made on the Grosso family— as far as anyone knew—which seemed to eliminate blackmail and extortion as motives, so who had started the rumors and why? All attempts to discover the identity of the blogger had failed.

A few pundits speculated it had to be Gina herself, trying to get back into the family, but that didn't make sense. If she knew she was Gina, why had she kept silent for so long, and why come forward now? Why not just go to the family and identify herself? A DNA test would easily verify her claim.

It was a fascinating conundrum, a regular whodunit with a bunch of pieces missing, and it got Dave thinking.

What kind of person would kidnap a baby? How could anyone steal an infant, only days old? It wasn't as if the child had been in an abusive environment. All the published reports indicated Dean and Patsy Grosso, while still teenagers at the time of the twins' births, were decent, God-fearing, loving parents with plenty of family support. What possible reason—except greed—could explain so heartless a crime?

Dave loved reading mysteries, both fictional and real. He loved trying to get into the mind of the bad guy, even when he hadn't yet figured out who the bad guy was. Here now was a real-life mystery involving NASCAR people he'd met. It couldn't get more interesting than that.

Dave opened the last of his father's journals, and the realization made him sad. When he finished it he would be saying goodbye to his dad again. Reading his cramped, sometimes nearly indecipherable handwriting was like having him there, whispering secrets in his ear.

He opened the volume. It was only half-filled. A week before his death, William Foster had attended a medical conference in Nashville where he'd been a featured speaker, delivering a paper on a new surgical technique for knee cartilage replacement and subsequent therapy. Apparently the presentation had been a big success, because he received several invitations to speak at other conferences.

Then Dave came upon an entry that baffled him. His father had met a man at the conference he called Jim, who claimed to know who had kidnapped Gina Grosso more than twenty years before. Dave scanned the remaining pages of the journal, looking for additional information. He found none.

How strange. How intriguing but also bewildering. It wasn't like his dad to be cute, to bring up a tantalizing subject then completely drop it. Had his intent been to follow up on it later, not knowing he would die before he got the chance?

Who was Jim? Why wasn't he further identified? His dad frequently mentioned his colleagues, but he was meticulous when discussing patients, using only their first names and maybe not even their real names. Did this mean Jim was or had been one of his patients? Did patients attend medical conferences? Could he have once been a patient of Dad's who was now attending the conference as a doctor or a nurse? Or maybe a therapist?

The most important question, of course, was if this guy knew who had kidnapped Gina Grosso, why hadn't he informed the authorities back when they were actively investigating the crime? Maybe he had talked to the police or the FBI and they'd had reason to dismiss him. Could the guy simply be a kook? Or had he come up with the information much later and didn't know what to do with it? Perhaps it was nothing more than suspicion or speculation, and he had no proof.

The statement to his father could have been the ravings of a drunk at the bar, Dave supposed, but if it that were true, why had his dad even bothered to note it in his journal?

Dave heard the grandfather clock in the hallway strike one. He'd lost track of time. Two thoughts kept going through his head as he brushed his teeth and climbed into bed. One was a question, the other a decision.

HE WAS WAITING FOR them at the Asheville airport.

"What's he doing here?" Nicole asked as she extended the handle on the oversize piece of luggage she'd taken with her to Chicago. Her flight home had been overbooked. The earliest confirmed reservation she could get wasn't until Tuesday afternoon, which meant she'd have to reschedule her patients for Monday and Tuesday. When Trey offered her a ride on his private plane she wasn't exactly delighted, but she could hardly turn it down. She'd called her brother to let him know about the change in plans, but she hadn't expected him to meet her at the airport.

"Worrywart," Trey mumbled. He thanked the ground crew member who'd unloaded their baggage and set it on the tarmac for pickup. Trey's was much smaller than Nicole's, but then his motor home was fully stocked. He didn't have to live out of a suitcase. "Maybe he's come out to welcome us back."

"Right."

Trey had seen very little of her over the weekend. He'd been racing and she'd been in the infield care center. Since he'd been spared injury when he crashed, he hadn't required her medical services. What he'd sought was her company, but she'd rejected his dinner invitations and every other social overture.

If Dave was aware of the chill between them, he gave no indication of it by his greeting.

"Sorry about the crash, man," he told Trey. "A really exciting race up to that point. Bad luck."

"Yeah," Trey agreed. "Another DNF. Luckily no one was hurt."

"What brings you out here?" Nicole asked warily. "Is something wrong? Are you having problems with your VNS?"

"Relax, sis. I'm fine." He shifted his glance to Trey. "You guys have time to go to the coffee shop and talk for a few minutes?"

"Sounds important." Trey glanced at Nicole for her concurrence. "Sure."

A minute later they'd settled into a booth. Nicole ordered a cup of decaf. Trey opted for iced tea. Dave requested a cola.

"So what's up?" Trey asked.

Dave thanked Nicole for giving him their father's journals, then told them about the entries concerning the kidnapping of Gina Grosso and their father's unexplained reference to a man named Jim. Nicole agreed it was curious.

"What are you planning to do with the information?" Trey asked.

"Take it to the FBI. I'll have to give them Dad's journal, of course. At least the last one."

"The FBI?" Nicole's eyebrows went up.

"They investigated the kidnapping when it happened," Dave explained. "Kidnapping's a federal crime, and since it involved the purported death of the victim, it's probably still considered an open case."

"But the baby's dead," she noted. "At least they thought she was. I know there's talk now about her being alive, but would that be enough for them to reopen a three-decades' old case?"

"The victim was believed to be dead, but the crimes committed against her, kidnapping and murder, weren't solved."

"You seem to have thought this all out," Trey remarked.

"I researched on the Internet today. Between watching the race, of course," he added hurriedly.

Trey chuckled. "Good for you. I know Jake McMasters, the P.I. who's investigating this case for the Grossos. I bet he'd be interested in this, too. I could contact him."

"Cool," Dave said, then went on. "I've decided something else, too. I've figured out what I want to do, what I want to study in school. Criminology. Now that I have a VNS, I bet I can go into law enforcement. What I really want is to become a profiler. I know I won't be able to do that right away. It may take years, but that's what I want to do."

"Law enforcement," Nicole repeated thoughtfully. "It never occurred to me that you might be interested in law enforcement. When did you decide this? You've never talked about becoming a cop or an FBI agent before."

"I've been thinking about it for a long time, but it was reading Dad's journals that convinced me it's what I really want to do. What kind of sick mind would steal a baby? I want to do what I can to stop people like that."

She smiled. "I think it's a great idea."

"You do?" He was incredulous.

She smiled at him, her eyebrows raised, then reached across the table and covered his hand with hers. He frowned with uncertainty. "Dave, why wouldn't I?" she asked. "You want to help people. You want to protect them. I think you will make a great profiler. You've got an analytical mind, plenty of intelligence. You're not afraid of hard work, and you're able to empathize with people. I think Mom and Dad would be very proud of your decision, too."

Trey nodded his agreement.

As she walked out of the shop a few minutes later, she could feel Trey's eyes on her back. He approved of her response to her brother. She appreciated that, but it wasn't enough.

CHAPTER NINETEEN

NICOLE'S CONTRACT with NASCAR for services in the infield care center was primarily for tracks on the East Coast, but there were exceptions, her attending the race in Chicago being one. The race the following weekend at Indianapolis, however, though farther east, was not on the list, and she decided to use the time to make up for her absence at the clinic the previous weekend.

She'd loved going to Indy years earlier with her parents and best friends Tara and Becky, right after NASCAR started racing there, soaking in the history, the drama and pageantry that were part of the oldest motor speedway in the world. She would have enjoyed attending this year, too, but it was probably as well she didn't. Better to keep her distance from Trey Sanford.

Hadn't this torturous situation all started with physical attraction? His handsome face. His well-toned body. The heat radiating off him when she locked her arm with his and snapped his shoulder back into place. The sound of his voice. The blue of his eyes.

Physical attraction.

Pheromones.

Hormones.

Disaster.

She'd thought he was someone special, fooled herself into falling in love with him, even though they were unsuited. Not physically unsuited. Those pheromones and hormones were working fine—too well, in fact. It was at the emotional and temperamental levels where they weren't compatible. He didn't respect her enough to make the right decision. Well, she didn't want or need a knight to rescue her from fire-eating dragons. Oh, she wouldn't object to him handing her a fire extinguisher now and then. In fact she'd appreciate the strong, outstretched hand of help, but she wanted to make her own choices, follow her own instincts, be her own person.

He was convinced it was his right, his obligation to be in control, to lord it over her. Well, there was a time and place for everything. Living one's life under the arbitrary whim of someone else's impulses wasn't her idea of happiness or fulfillment.

Trey Sanford was the wrong man for her. She needed to stay away from him. Starting with Indianapolis.

THE TRACK AT INDY was sort of a love/hate affair for NASCAR drivers, teams and fans. Trey loved it. Ethan and Adam hated it. It wasn't an easy track to drive. The straightaways were flat, the turns were banked a mere nine degrees. This speedway wasn't designed for stock cars. The concept of stock cars hadn't even existed when it was built at the beginning of the last century. At a time when automobiles were still competing with horses, fast was anything over ten miles an hour, and ten miles without a breakdown was a minor miracle.

"The key," Trey told his team in the garage area Friday morning while they were preparing Car No. 483 for practice laps, "is going to be the starting lineup."

Indy's two-and-a-half-mile length made it one of the longest tracks in the series, but the roadway was narrow. The flat straightaways made it fast, but its sharp turns made it terrifying for drivers and spectators. Passing was a bear.

"Give me the juice," Trey said, "and I'll get the position."

Brave words. He was still trailing badly behind the leader as they approached the Chase for the NASCAR Sprint Cup. Victory here at Indy, however, could put him in serious contention, not just point-wise but also morale-wise. As a shadow crossed the open garage doorway, he looked up and was startled to see Dave standing there. Instantly he searched for Nicole.

Trey nodded to the boy, concluded his remarks with his engine chief and made his way to his visitor.

"I didn't expect to see you here," he said, then remembered to put a smile on his face. He didn't want the kid to think he wasn't welcome. "Is your sister with you?"

"She's working this weekend at the clinic."

"Oh." Even he could hear the disappointment in his voice.

Dang it, he couldn't seem to stop thinking about her. He'd told her he loved her, something he'd said to no other woman, but it wasn't enough. Nothing he said seemed to make an impression. He didn't understand what more he could do, what he was supposed to do. How he felt about her didn't matter if she didn't love him back, and obviously she didn't.

Was there any way he could earn her love? He couldn't see how. Everything he did seemed to backfire.

"So what are you doing here?"

"I came to see the race," Dave replied, sounding perplexed that the question was asked.

"I mean, what about your swimming tryouts? Weren't they this weekend?"

"The prelims were held yesterday. I didn't make the cut. I guess I was still too sore from the implant surgery to put full power into my strokes."

"I'm sorry." Trey felt guilty for pushing the kid into the VNS surgery. Bad timing. On the other hand waiting would have been miserable for him.

"No regrets," Dave assured him. "I can try out for the swimming team next year. The VNS is more important than any old scholarship."

Trey agreed in principle and hoped Nicole did, too. "If your sister isn't with you, how did you get here?"

Dave grinned. "I flew. I tried to book a direct flight from Charlotte, but they were full. The closest I could get was Chicago. They didn't have any flights available, either, so I rented a car there and drove."

"Whoa, you drove here all the way from Chicago? In a rented car?"

"It's only a couple hundred miles. I had to purchase extra high-risk insurance, though, because I'm not twenty-one." Dave's casual shrug indicated it was no big deal. "You don't have to worry about the VNS," he added. "It's working fine."

Trey shook his head. "I wasn't worried about the VNS as much as the traffic. Chicago is a lot busier than Brevard or Charlotte."

It was Dave's turn to laugh. "Hey, you gave me the Sanford Experience, remember? Chicago was a piece of cake, sort of fun actually, and the Interstate was a breeze, especially when I drafted behind an eighteen-wheeler."

Trey cringed and hoped he hadn't created a monster. If anything happened to Dave, Nicole would never forgive him; he'd never forgive himself. A man-to-man discussion was called for later. Trey noted the credentials dangling from a lanyard around the kid's neck. "Where'd you get the passes?"

"I called Ethan from Chicago and asked him if he could get me in. When we met in California he told me to call him if I ever needed anything."

Ethan would. He could be a taskmaster but he was a soft touch when it came to young people. "Why didn't you call me?"

"I wanted it to be a surprise."

Familiar words. *I wanted it to be a surprise.* The image of Nicole's face rose up before him. Not surprise on it but an expression of affront for not being consulted beforehand about the trip to San Meloso.

"Where are you staying?"

"I don't know yet," Dave admitted with a shrug. "I figured I'd go to a hotel."

"On one of the biggest race weekends of the year? You must be kidding. You won't find anything. Okay, you can stay in my motor home. Have to sleep on the couch, though."

For the first time Dave looked embarrassed. "I didn't mean—"

Trey gave him an elbow in the ribs. "Don't worry about it. Next time, though, see if you can plan ahead a little better. What did your sister say when you told her you were coming here?" Too bad she hadn't decided to come with him. Of course, then Dave wouldn't be sleeping on his couch, and if he had his way, she wouldn't be, either.

"I didn't tell her."

Trey stared at him. "You didn't tell your sister you were coming here." A host of thoughts ran through his head. He took a moment to collect them. "So where did you get the money for the airline ticket?"

"From my money-market account," Dave replied.

"From your inheritance money."

Trey wasn't sure how much was in the fund, but if it was enough to put him through college, it wasn't chump change. Whatever the amount, it wouldn't last long if Dave dipped into it every time he wanted to go somewhere on the spur of the moment. Money, however, wasn't the issue at the moment.

"Why didn't you tell your sister where you were going?"

Dave shifted from one foot to the other, clearly aware he'd acted wrongly, and with that silent acknowledgment, Trey realized something else.

Decisions have consequences.

Finally, he understood. Whether a decision was right or wrong, it had tentacles that reached out and affected other people, often with unintended consequences that went well beyond the immediate situation.

Taking Nicole and Dave to Mexico could have been fun. For Dave it had been a new adventure, the beginning of a new life, a happy memory. For Nicole it had been a trap. Sure she wanted the best for her brother and if that included a VNS, she wanted that for him, too. But after being such an important part of his life for so long she expected—and had the right to expect—to be consulted on the decision that concerned his welfare, not confronted with it. That Trey hadn't intended to exclude her didn't mitigate the fact that he had. If anything, it made it worse. He'd taken her for granted.

Picking up the tab on Dave's VNS could have been a precious gift. For Dave it was. For Nicole, it had been an insult bordering on humiliation, as if she couldn't afford to pay for her brother's medical treatment.

Giving Dave a car for his birthday could have been a generous present. Dave certainly enjoyed it. For Nicole it represented disrespect, almost a slap in the face, considering driving had been such a big issue between her and her brother. *I'm afraid of what your love will do to me.* My God, what had he done?

He'd told her he loved her, and it was true, but he

realized now with dazzling clarity that his actions had belied his words. His love was real, but it was also selfish. What he thought he had done for her had been for himself, because it made him feel good. He had been trying to earn her thanks, not her love.

Why hadn't he told her he wanted to take them to San Meloso? Even better, why hadn't he *asked* her if she wanted to go there? Had he really thought she would have rejected an opportunity to improve her brother's life?

If the cost of the VNS was an issue, why hadn't he offered to help defray the expense—or even to lend her the money—instead of cavalierly telling her he was picking up the tab for everything?

When he decided to buy Dave a car for his birthday, why hadn't he talked to her about it? Why hadn't he asked her to help him choose the car? What fun they could have had car shopping together.

And the Sanford Experience! Giving it to Dave had been a great idea, especially if it helped the teenager work his way through Chicago traffic, but why the deuce hadn't he thought of offering it to Nicole, too? He could have been her driver, taken her out on the track and let her experience racing the way he did.

Idiot! Stupid, selfish idiot.

CHAPTER TWENTY

"YOU CAN STAY WITH ME," Trey reiterated, "but first you have to call your sister, let her know where you are."

"I'm eighteen," Dave argued. "I don't need her permission to go wherever I want."

This was the closest the kid had come to answering him back. Maybe his idol status was slipping. Trey took a moment before he responded.

"This isn't about permission," he explained. "It's about respect. We owe respect and consideration to the people who love us. It's one way for us to show we're worthy of their love." He couldn't believe what he was saying or how he was saying it. What was even more remarkable was that he knew it was true.

Dave tightened his lips in a sulk, making Trey realize the boy still harbored a good deal of resentment toward his sister and that he needed to do some growing up. *Welcome to the club.*

"Whether you agree with all her decisions in the past isn't important at the moment," he continued. "Whether those decisions were the right ones isn't important." He waited for the young man to raise his head and look at him. "She did what she thought was best for you, Dave. She sacrificed a lot to give you the best life she could because she loves you. I'm sure right now she's worried sick about you.

The least you owe her is the courtesy of telling her where you are and that you're okay."

He nodded. "I'll call her." He turned to leave.

Tray grabbed his arm. "I also suggest," he added, "that you apologize to her for making her worry."

Dave sucked in a breath. "I will."

Trey emitted a quiet sigh of relief as he watched the tall, lanky boy-man snake his way along the side of the garages. Growing up was a bumpy road, and Dave had a couple of extra deep potholes to contend with, but he'd make it.

"Ready?"

Trey jerked around to face his crew chief. The deafening sounds of unmuffled high-performance engines being gunned and goosed came rushing back like a bone-rattling assault. He swiped his right wrist across his upper chest— as a precaution. It was time to run his qualifying laps.

THE SIXTH POSITION IN the lineup was good, Trey assured himself, as he made his way to his motor home late that evening. He and the team had spent the past few hours discussing options and strategies for Sunday's race. How many pit stops and when to take them? Should they alternate two- and four-tire changes or go with four every time? Indy was a nearly flat track; the lateral wear on tires, inside and out, was much greater than on a well-banked course. Four tire changes, then. Where were the best places for passing? They reviewed the lineup and identified who they thought would likely be the main contenders. This competition was far more of a game of chess than checkers. All the planning and strategizing would go out the window when the green flag came down. Nothing ever ended up the way it was planned. Every decision, small or large, had ripple effects, a microcosm of life.

Trey greeted people in his trek across the infield.

Turning on the charm, waving to folks who called out, some of them complete strangers, shaking a few hands, was automatic, robotic, compulsive.

It's about respect. We owe respect and consideration to the people who love us. It's how we show we're worthy of their love.

Why hadn't he understood that lesson earlier? He loved Nicole, but he'd failed to show her respect or even the courtesy of consideration. He'd made decisions that affected her life and her brother's without consulting her. He'd second-guessed her decisions, humiliated her in front of her brother. *Nice going, champ!* Great way to impress a woman.

He'd given Dave the access code to his motor home, so he wasn't surprised to find the kid already inside, long legs stretched out on the leather couch, a soft drink in one hand, his cell phone in the other. He looked up.

"Got to go, Jen. Trey just walked in. Talk to you later. Hey, man, sixth in the lineup is good." He holstered the tiny instrument.

"Did you call your sister?"

"Yep, got her as she was going out to dinner with that doctor she works with, John Something-or-other."

John Preston. Trey's stomach muscles tightened. He remembered the square-jawed pediatrician, the guy with the predatory gleam in his eyes every time he looked at Nicole. "Preston."

Dave picked up the TV remote and un-muted the sound. Pundits were making their prognostications for the race ahead. They unanimously agreed Trey Sanford was a wild card.

"Crap," Trey muttered to himself, retrieved a small bottle of juice from the refrigerator, took a slug and plopped down in the easy chair at the foot of the couch.

The images and sounds coming from the hi-def screen on the wall had ceased to make any impressions. "How is she?"

His eyes still glued to the screen, where they were analyzing Trey's qualification lap, it took Dave an irritatingly long moment to answer. "She's cool,'" he mumbled distractedly. "Wondered where I had gone off to is all."

A minute went by. Racing sounds emanated from the screen. Faces appeared. Talking heads.

"Did she ask about me?"

"Nope. Didn't have time to. John What's-his-name was waiting. Said she had to run."

Trey's heart sank. *I've lost her.* The ache in his chest was filled with regret and self-loathing. He'd found her and lost her. He deserved to after the way he'd treated her. He stood up, paced across the carpet in front of the screen, back again. He'd screwed up, but he wasn't about to let her go. He'd fight. Wasn't that what men did, fight for their women? But how?

He could challenge John to a duel, except he didn't have a sword and wouldn't know how to use it if he did. A bare-knuckles fistfight? It would be hard to drive with a couple of broken hands, and he didn't imagine the good doctor would want to damage his paws, either. Besides, John was a good two inches taller, at least thirty pounds heavier and, from the looks of him, it was all solid muscle.

No, Trey decided, he had to do something else to win her back. Something to prove he was worthy of her love.

NICOLE SAT IN THE PLUSH upholstered chair, the fingertips of her right hand on the base of her wineglass. An excellent vintage, a robust, spicy red with a variety of complex flavors subtly intermingled. At least that's what she'd been told. She normally appreciated a good Bordeaux, but for some reason tonight it might as well have been Chianti.

She had ordered sliced filet mignon, which was prepared flambé at tableside and came with a rich and flavorful brown mushroom sauce. Perfectly prepared, expertly served and absolutely delicious. Of that she had no doubt, but even this fine French cuisine didn't seem to appeal to her tonight.

John sat across from her, cutting enthusiastically into a prime porterhouse. The sports jacket he was wearing was expertly tailored and probably cost as much as the dress she had on tonight, an electric blue A-line that had been hanging in her closet for ages for lack of an occasion to wear it.

"That was quite a mess this afternoon." John was referring to a construction worker who'd tumbled off a roof. His fall had been broken when his right leg became snagged in the building's scaffolding. The interruption had probably saved his life, but at a cost. "I saw the X-rays. It's a miracle you were able to save the leg, considering the number of bone fragments and the extent of vascular damage he suffered. He's lucky you were there to work on him."

She didn't think she'd done anything any other competent orthopedist couldn't have done, but she smiled in appreciation of the compliment.

"He may not think so when he starts rehab," she remarked. "I was able to put all the pieces back together again, but the rest will be up to him, a classic case of use it or lose it."

She forked up another sliver of beef. John was spending a fortune on this meal. The least she could do was eat it. She loved her work and was usually eager to talk about it, especially with a fellow professional, but tonight she wasn't in the mood to discuss mangled limbs and blown joints. She didn't want to focus on her world, because when she did she thought about people who were no longer in it—Trey and Dave. It wasn't logical, of course. They weren't her patients, didn't have orthopedic problems she had to deal with. They were separate, independent individuals, and she was a complete person without them.

She asked John why he'd gone into pediatrics.

"For the smile." A good answer. She knew exactly what he meant.

He was wonderful with children. He was incredibly patient and gentle, even with the little terrors he sometimes treated, who fought him every step of the way.

"It must be heartbreaking sometimes, though," she observed.

He shrugged. "You do your part and hope it's enough. It isn't always, as you know, and when you fail it hurts, but so far the victories have outnumbered the defeats, the smiles have outweighed the tears. As long as the ratio stays that way, I'll stick with it."

The conversation shifted to hobbies and pastimes. She wasn't interested in talking about the athletic opportunities she'd given up, about NASCAR or old books, so she focused the discussion on him. He'd played basketball in high school—no surprise there—and received an athletic scholarship in college. "At six-four," he added with a self-deprecating smile, "I was usually the shortest player on the court. Being the little guy was often an advantage, though, at least temporarily, because I was underestimated."

By the time he had polished off his steak, she'd eaten about half of her filet. He noticed but didn't say anything. Their plates were removed. She accepted the offer of espresso and would have turned down dessert until their server mentioned crème brûlée. John ordered the same.

The evening passed pleasantly enough. She liked John. Charming and easygoing, his sophistication wasn't forced or pretentious but the natural good manners of a man who was comfortable with himself. She wondered why he was still single, why some equally sophisticated beauty hadn't gobbled him up. Maybe she had. Maybe he was divorced or widowed. If so, he was very good at keeping his private life private. Had he been around six months earlier, she reflected, she might easily have fallen for him. Maybe she still could, but not tonight.

At her door she could feel him waiting for her to invite him in. She was hungry for company, male company, but not his, not tonight.

She smiled and thanked him for an enjoyable evening in a way she hoped made it clear their time together had come to an end. She put her key in the lock and cracked the door open when he put his hand on her forearm. Reflexively stiffening, she turned toward him.

"I've enjoyed spending time with you, Nicole. I hope we can do it again." He gave her an understanding grin. "When you have more of an appetite." Then he tilted her chin up and touched his lips to hers.

She couldn't say she was stunned or even displeased by his action, nor, despite her initial reaction to his physical contact, did she feel threatened by it. Under other circumstances she would have participated in the kiss, but not tonight. Fortunately his advance ended with the overture. When she didn't immediately respond, he lingered for only a moment, then broke off the kiss. His disappointment was palpable, but he didn't seem discouraged or disheartened.

With a rueful smile he stepped back, raised his hand in a courteous salute, wished her a good night and trotted down the porch steps. On the path he turned back briefly to wave again, then proceeded to his Italian sports car at curbside. A few seconds later the street was quiet.

Nicole let herself into the house, locked the door behind her and leaned against it. Tears welled in her eyes. An unbearable loneliness weighed her down. Not for John. She'd all but forgotten him. For Trey. He should have been the one eating the porterhouse across from her, sharing her custard, kissing her at the door. He should be at her side this very minute helping her turn off the downstairs lights and accompanying her up to her bedroom.

She'd been unfair to John. All evening he'd been trying to entertain her, entice her into appreciating him as a man instead of a doctor, and in that he'd succeeded. He was a sweet, gentle man who loved kids, who liked to see them smile. She'd played her part, nodded, smiled at appropriate intervals, carried on a conversation she had no memory of, while all the time her mind had been on Trey and Dave.

She'd tried not to overreact when Dave called to tell her he was with Trey at Indy. She'd lost them both, the two most important men in her life. Dave resented her for being overprotective, and Trey…he seemed to agree, enough that he didn't trust her judgment when it came to her brother. Resentment and low esteem were big obstacles to overcome.

With time she'd get Dave back. He'd be off to college soon. On his own. He wouldn't have to face his CFS every day. He'd have time to think and make his own decisions. Maybe he wouldn't find them as easy as he imagined. Maybe he wouldn't always make the right ones. Who ever did?

What about Trey? She loved him, too. Loved him in a way she'd never imagined she could love someone. Yet…he didn't respect her. He made decisions for her and expected her to be grateful.

As she lay in bed, her body restless, unable to fall asleep, her mind churned.

Trey had asked what she would have done about the trip

to Santa Ysidra if he'd let her make the decision. Of course she would have agreed eventually. In the meantime, though, she would have demanded assurances no one could give. As a doctor she should have known better.

She sat up in bed, all at once seeing what she hadn't been able to see before—that she was as controlling as Trey was.

CHAPTER TWENTY-ONE

TREY SAT ON THE EDGE of the bed and looked over at the clock. Eight forty-five. He rarely slept this late. Even as a kid, when everyone else wanted to laze in bed, he was champing at the bit to get on with the day.

Well, it looked like he'd slept in this morning.

Wait. The last time he'd glanced over at the clock on his bedside table it had been 7:50 a.m. He clearly remembered stretching and starting to get up. Now the digital readout said 8:45. What had happened to the intervening fifty-five minutes?

He ran his wrist across his chest. Surely...

He checked the clock again. No question about the time. Eight forty-five.

Had he lain back down and fallen asleep? It would be unusual for him, but...why didn't he remember waking up the second time?

He distinctly recalled waking, sitting up on the side of the bed and looking at the clock. Seven-fifty. The next thing he knew he was still sitting there, but this time the clock said eight forty-five.

Could he... Was it possible that he'd...?

This was exactly what happened during one of his absence seizures. He started to do something, a conversation, a routine task, and stopped. Time came to a standstill, then he resumed exactly where he had left off, except there was a missing block of time. Usually a minute or two, especially if there were other people around to jolt him out of his catatonic state, but there was no one here now. He could easily have sat on the side of the bed for fifty minutes without moving, without any stimulus to disrupt his trance-like spell.

He hadn't had a seizure in six years, not since he'd received the VNS. When he was at Santa Ysidra with Dave and Nicole, Dr. Price had interrogated it. The device was working perfectly. The battery would need changing in another year or so, but Denise had assured him it had plenty of dependable power left.

Could he have fallen back to sleep in a sitting position? He did have a crick in his neck, which he couldn't remember ever having before. He hadn't slept very well last night. He kept thinking about Nicole, thinking about her going to dinner with her tall, strapping medical colleague. The two of them would have had plenty in common, plenty to talk about. When "Big John" took her home, did he kiss her good-night? Did she kiss him back? Where exactly had they been when they kissed? On the front porch? In the hallway? In her bedroom?

Trey remembered jolting awake from that nightmare around two o'clock. When he'd finally gotten back to sleep, it had been more of the same. He'd been mysteriously standing in the corner of her bedroom watching John undress her. He'd tried to yell at her not to let him touch her that way, but she hadn't heard him, and he'd sprung up in bed again. That had been around four o'clock.

The next time he looked at the clock, it read 7:50. He certainly had a good excuse for being exhausted.

Had he fallen back to sleep? Or had he had a seizure? The uncertainty was nerve-racking.

"It doesn't make any difference," he muttered into the

mirror as he was shaving. "The VNS takes care of me, and I can give it an extra nudge, if it needs it." *During waking hours.*

What were his options?

He could assume it was not a seizure. Given his history over the past six years and Dr. Price's recent evaluation, it probably wasn't, and if it wasn't, there was no reason he couldn't drive today and tomorrow. He could call Dr. Price on Monday and talk to her about it, even fly down to San Meloso if she wanted to check him out again. She might even want to replace the battery in his device sooner than scheduled as a precaution.

Or...

If he'd had a seizure and not just nodded off after a restless night, he didn't dare climb behind the wheel of a car. If he was vulnerable to seizures—would the one this morning be considered a waking seizure or a sleeping seizure?—he would be putting himself and everyone else on the track in danger. It would be immoral, and he'd never forgive himself if someone got hurt.

He could have it checked out today to be absolutely sure. That would mean no practice laps on a track that cried for as many practice laps as he could squeeze in. There was also the complication of trying to explain to his team why he wasn't around before a critical race. Dicey. Yet...

He finished dressing and with the bedroom door still closed called his brother.

"Something's come up," he told Adam, "something I need to attend to right away."

"Dammit, Trey, this is not the time...." He took an audible breath. Anger hardened his words. "You're really trying my patience. Perhaps I ought to remind you that just because your name is Sanford—" Adam's cadence suddenly slowed "—doesn't entitle you..."

As the last word was being spoken, Trey recognized that his brother had finally caught on, and in that single syllable he heard both awareness and panic. They never said "seizure disorder" or "epilepsy" on the phone or in public. Even at home it had become "it" and nothing more.

"Look—" Trey struggled to keep his tone both frank and casual "—Mom's pacemaker will probably check out fine, but there is an outside chance I may not make it back in time for the race tomorrow. If that happens, have Shelley Green—" she was their driver in the NASCAR Nationwide Series "—take the wheel for me."

"You're absolutely sure this is necessary?"

Trey knew the spot he was putting his brother in. Adam would have to explain the last-minute substitution to both teams without disclosing the real reason Trey wasn't available. In a season when morale seemed to be walking a tightrope, this was not good.

"Keep me posted," Adam said after a moment's pause. "Do you need help?"

"Dave's here. I'll ask him to come along." Then Trey added, "He's had the Sanford Experience."

With a hint of humor, Adam noted, "He's all set, then." Another brief hesitation. "Good luck."

Trey's next call was to Dr. Price. Anyone listening in would think they were talking about his mother's occasional sleeping disorder and problems with her pacemaker—a pacemaker she didn't have.

The neurologist's message was clear. *Don't panic.*

She directed him to take "her" to a private hospital in Indianapolis where a colleague would discreetly run the appropriate tests and in consultation with Dr. Price, make any electronic or medication adjustments that might be appropriate.

Trey's big question was whether he'd be able to race the next day, but he knew there was no point in asking it.

He went to his living room where Dave was still zonked out on the couch and roused him. "I need you to do me a favor."

NICOLE'S YEARS IN MEDICAL school, internship and residency had taught her to get along on very little sleep. Saturday morning when she rolled out of bed the sun was barely pinking the sky above the mountain ridges. She felt as though she'd already worked a seventy-two-hour shift and run a marathon during her breaks. She dragged herself into the shower, set the water temperature several degrees cooler than she liked it to get her blood circulating and, once dressed, hurried down to the kitchen to put on coffee and call the airport.

She wasn't surprised to learn every flight to Indianapolis was filled. This was a big weekend at the famous track. Her chances of finding a hotel room were probably even worse, but for now the important thing was being there. She could probably sleep on the floor of wherever Dave was holed up, if it came to that. He wouldn't like it, but then, neither would she.

She packed an overnight bag, small enough to hand carry, filled an insulated mug with hot, strong coffee, got in her car and hightailed it to the airport. The agent at the ticket counter confirmed that every seat into Indianapolis was taken. Maybe she should do what Dave did, fly into another city and drive.

"I can put you on standby," the agent said. "It could be a long wait, but—"

"Let's do it." She experienced an odd sense of liberation at being so impetuous.

She was number nine on the waiting list for the first

flight out. She wasn't called, but she advanced closer to the top of the list for the next one. She resisted contacting Gaby Colson, Trey's PR rep, until eight o'clock, then told her she was flying in but didn't know when. Could she arrange for infield and garage passes? She could and would.

"One other thing," Nicole implored. "Don't tell Trey or my brother I'm coming. I'd like it to be a surprise."

Her name was finally called for the 2:12 flight. She didn't relax until the plane lifted off. When she landed, she had the further challenge of getting to the track. She was inquiring about the availability of ground transportation when a woman overheard her and offered her a lift with her husband and daughter. They'd leased the last pickup, a crew cab, the rental company had available. Nicole accepted with alacrity.

As INSTRUCTED, DAVE parked near the hospital's staff entrance on the north side of the medical complex. A security guard inside the doorway stopped them immediately. Trey gave the name he'd been told to use and requested Dr. Fischer be informed of his arrival. The neurologist was waiting when the staff elevator door opened on the sixth floor two minutes later. He was a slender man of medium height in his late fifties or early sixties with thinning gray hair combed straight back.

"Dr. Price has apprised me of the situation," he said, once they were alone. "We'll take the usual battery of blood tests, run an EKG, then we'll get a CT scan of your head. I'll also interrogate your VNS to ensure it's functioning properly. If those tests prove normal, we'll do an EEG, which, as you know, means an overnight stay."

Trey agreed. He had introduced Dave when they first met. "Where can he stay?"

"We have special arrangements with the hotel across the road for families of patients."

"Cool," said Dave. Another new experience for the kid, Trey thought, staying in a hotel by himself. What would Nicole think of that?

Trey called Adam, confirmed he would not be returning that afternoon, then rolled up his sleeve for the first jab by the phlebotomist.

"WHAT DO YOU MEAN they're not here?"

Nicole had gone to Trey's motor home and received no answer. Okay, no surprise. She'd called Dave's cell but was immediately switched to voice mail. From there she'd found her way to the garage area and talked to Ethan. Adam had informed him that morning that something had come up, that Trey had to leave and might not return in time for the race the next day. Ethan was prepping Shelley Green in case he didn't.

"He had an emergency," Adam told her twenty minutes later. "Your brother went with him."

"What kind of an emergency?"

They were alone in Adam's motor home, where they had absolute privacy. "He thinks he may have had an...episode."

It took a moment for the words to register. "Trey had a seizure?" Dread cascaded through her. This couldn't be happening. "But his VNS—"

"He's gone to have it checked."

"Where? I have to go to him, be with him."

"I honestly don't know," Adam told her. She doubted he was as cool about the development as he was pretending. The future of Sanford Racing could well hang in the balance of what the test produced, aside from the fact they were talking about his brother. Adam could be hard-nosed, but family was important to him. "Dr. Price probably knows," he went on. "Whether she'll tell you—"

"When will he be back?"

"I don't know that, either. Where are you staying?"

"What? Oh." She raised her shoulders and lowered them. "I don't know. Haven't gotten that far yet." She'd never gone off so unprepared in her life and look what it had gotten her. Stranded. "A hotel, I guess."

"You won't find anything within fifty miles of here. You can spend the night in Trey's motor home."

"So you're sure he's not coming back tonight." She sounded accusatory. Fortunately he didn't take offense.

"Nicole. Relax. Enjoy the place. It's well stocked. If you need anything, call me." He gave her his cell number, which she entered into hers.

Relax. Sure.

CHAPTER TWENTY-TWO

"WE'RE ON OUR WAY back now," Trey told his brother over the phone while he pointed out a road sign to Dave. They turned at the next corner onto the street that would take them to the highway. "The situation has been resolved. How's my car doing?"

"Waiting for you," Adam said. "Shelley's on standby to run practice laps this morning if you're not here in time. No problems?"

"Everything's fine."

Adam let out an audible sigh of relief. "The team's going to be glad to see you. I told them there was a family emergency but didn't specify what it was."

"They bought that?"

"Not really, and they're unhappy about being left in the dark. One guy wanted to know why I wasn't taking care of it, if it was a family emergency. We can do without a team owner, but not without a driver."

"That must have made you feel good," Trey quipped.

"A couple of people asked if Mom was okay, and a few seem to have jumped to the conclusion this *family emergency*—" he said it in a mocking tone "—is about you and your girlfriend in Mexico."

Trey laughed softly.

"I wish I could enjoy the humor with you," Adam said.

"Nerves, not humor, brother. What am I going to tell them?"

"I called Mom. She had been planning to come to the race but has agreed to stay home."

"She's never missed a race at Indy. I can't believe—"

"For heaven's sake, Trey, she's your mother. Of course she understands. Better call her as soon as you can and let her know you're all right. One other thing." There was a momentary pause. "I just want you to know nobody is blaming you for this. You didn't choose any of it. I'm proud of the way you've taken the high road in dealing with it, but I think we're going to have to reexamine how we handle it in the future."

"Thanks, and I agree, but not right now. Let's get through this race first."

"By the way, your other girlfriend, the real one," Adam said with a chuckle in his voice, "showed up yesterday."

"Nicole?" At the mention of his sister, Dave shot him a sharp glance from behind the wheel.

"I let her stay in your motor home last night. She wasn't a happy camper."

He swiped his wrist across his chest. "Does she know?"

"Yes."

"I'll see you in about an hour." He shut the phone and snapped it onto his belt holster.

Dave looked over. "Is everything okay? What was that about Nicole?"

"She's at the track. Came in yesterday afternoon." He waited for her brother to make a comment, but he didn't.

Dave did a good job of maneuvering them through the snarl of traffic that jammed access to the race track. Fifty minutes after leaving the hospital, he was parking the car in the infield.

They walked to the motor home. Trey had started up the

steps when the door flew open and Nicole, arms akimbo, a Valkyrie on the warpath, glared down at them.

Trey's chest pounded.

"Where have you two been?" she challenged.

"Hold it right there!" Dave exploded from behind Trey. "Who the hell do you think you are, showing up here demanding explanations? You have no damn right—"

"Dave," Trey growled without looking at him. He couldn't take his eyes off her. Any power he thought he might have had over his body, over his heart, was fiction now. Everyone else faded into the background. He saw only her, felt only the thrumming of hormone-charged blood heating and pooling.

"Cool it," he muttered, no longer sure at whom or about what.

"It's time for her to back off, to stop expecting everybody to answer to her. It's none of her damn business where—"

"Calm down." Trey continued to stare at her. She'd come. To see him or her brother? It didn't matter. She was here, standing on the steps of his home. "And watch your manners."

Dave mumbled something under his breath, turned and stalked away.

In silence Nicole watched him leave while Trey continued to observe her. She had circles under her eyes. The result of a sleepless night? Had she worried about him? He had to get a move on. There was a race to win. He mounted the last two steps, edged past her and entered the motor home. *His* motor home, but it was filled with her scent. She closed the door behind her and gazed anxiously at him, as if she expected him to tell her to get out.

"I need to get over to the garage," he said in a voice that was both informative and strangely pleading. "While I'm changing, I'll explain to you what's been going on."

"I didn't mean to be so—"

"Such a CFS?" He laughed nervously. "Are you going to come into the bedroom and watch me change or wait out here?" He swallowed the amusement that bubbled up inside him at the expression on her face. Not shock so much as temptation. Maybe all is not lost, he thought. Then he realized the effect the idea was having on him. He was a grown man. He should be able to control his libido, but he wasn't.

"I'll wait out here," she mumbled.

"Probably a wise choice."

SHE'D BEEN SITTING on the stool closest to the bedroom door and reaching for the coffee mug on the marble countertop when she'd heard feet ascending the outside steps a few minutes earlier. Her heart had thumped when she realized it had to be him at the door, and now that she'd confirmed it, now that she'd seen and heard him it continued to pound audibly in her ears. She abandoned the coffee. She didn't need caffeine with him so close. She didn't even have to be in the room with him to picture him unbuttoning his shirt, slipping it off his broad shoulders, retrieving his uniform from the closet and climbing into it.

"So I called Dr. Price," he was saying from behind the door he'd left ajar.

The image of him standing bare legged, bare chested in the bedroom had distracted her from his words.

"Start again," she requested. "I missed what you said the first time."

He poked his head around the door frame, a fresh T-shirt dangling from one hand. She could see his bare chest, the subtle scars above and below his left collarbone, the play of lean muscles beneath them. "I said I thought I might have had a seizure."

He retreated back inside and continued to sing out the chronicle of events that had transpired.

"Dave showing up when he did was a lifesaver," she heard him say. "If he hadn't been here I would have had to ask someone else to drive me to the hospital, and that would have complicated the situation even further."

"He stayed at the hospital with you?" That would explain his cell being turned off.

Trey emerged from the bedroom fully garbed. "At a nearby hotel. I offered to pay for it this morning, but he'd already taken care of the bill. By the way, he's a darn good driver. You can relax on that score."

"At the moment my brother isn't my primary concern. The tests," she prompted. "What did they show?"

"I didn't have a seizure. The VNS is working fine. The EKG and EEG, as well as the other tests, indicate I have not had an episode of any kind. I'm in the best of health."

If looks counted, she agreed. "Then what happened?"

"I fell back to sleep." He grinned. "It's as simple as that. I started to get up yesterday morning after a restless night and dozed off again, sitting on the side of the bed. Nothing mysterious. Nothing sinister. Just plain old fatigue."

She wanted to ask him why his night had been restless, but there was no time. He strode directly to the door, opened it and held it for her.

Minutes later she'd lost him—to several fans who wanted autographs, to a reporter who wanted his predictions for the day's race. To his brother and teammates. His reply was the same to all of them: "I'm going to win."

SHE'D COME HERE TO make peace with her brother and with Trey, and within the first minute of seeing them she'd managed to make matters worse. She ought to leave, return to her clinic, help people mend their damaged bodies, accept another date with John Preston. He was a nice guy, a good doctor, loved kids, and if the relationship between them matured into more than a professional friendship, he'd no doubt treat her right, with consideration and respect. He was handsome and thoughtful, doing well in his profession…

But he didn't excite her, not the way Trey made her pulse jump. He didn't fill her mind and heart when he wasn't around. She didn't wonder what he was doing when they weren't together. She didn't yearn for his company when they were separated. For all his flaws, Trey resonated in her, stirred a tension that filled her with joy when she was with him, made her feel incomplete when she wasn't.

No other man compared with Trey.

Adam invited her to watch the practice laps from the top of the hauler. Dave was already in place. At first brother and sister merely acknowledged each other's presence with a nod, but during the break, Dave came over to her.

"Sorry about what I said, sis."

Another apology? The second in two days. Had Trey put him up to this?

She cracked a soft smile. "I'm sorry, too, Dave, sorry I always come on so strong." Pause. "Trey tells me you're a pretty good driver."

"I'm okay, I guess." Humility became him and the sincerity of it prompted respect. She couldn't help wondering if Trey was at least in part responsible for this new step toward maturity. He was a great big brother. He'd make a wonderful father.

Her smile broadened into a grin. "When a NASCAR driver says you're good, you're good. I'm glad. Are you considering taking up racing?"

He gazed at her in shock, then genuine amusement brightened his face. "Me? No way. The Sanford Experience was fantastic. I enjoyed every minute of it, but no, I don't want to be a race car driver. I want to go into law enforcement, like I told you, be a profiler."

She continued to smile. "Help catch the bad guys, eh?"

"If I can."

"You'll be good. And there's always the Sanford Experience if one of them tries to get away."

They both laughed, and Nicole knew they would overcome whatever obstacles might lie between them. In spite of everything, even her being a CFS, they'd be there for each other.

They watched the race together, sometimes from the hauler, for a few minutes from atop the war wagon, from behind the wall during pit stops. They watched and cheered. Once, without realizing it, she grabbed Dave's hand and squeezed it, and he squeezed back.

TREY MOVED FROM SIXTH place to third within the first few laps, battled with Will Branch for second, took it, then trailed Freddie Harris for the next four laps. Harris had a blowout on the backstretch but managed to maneuver onto the grassy infield without incident. Trey led the pack for eight laps, until Barney Constantine edged ahead on the approach to Turn Three. After the first pit stop, Trey led for six more laps, took a tap by Finnegan Jarvis and nearly spun out but succeeded in holding on to second place.

Another game of cat and mouse followed the second pit stop. Trey and Haze Clifford traded the number one position for five laps, then Trey advanced, established some distance with the rest of the pack and took the lead position.

"Nordstrom is moving up," Ethan advised Trey over the intercom. "He's in fourth at the moment."

Nordstrom had started out in the eighth position, run into suspension problems early on and had fallen into the second pack by the middle of the race. The problem seemed to get resolved during the fourth pit stop, because after that he started pressing forward, slipped into the lead pack and continued to make steady progress. Nordstrom was a tough competitor. Trey knew he wouldn't be content with anything less than first place.

"Yellow flag. Yellow flag."

"What's going on?" From his vantage point Trey couldn't tell.

"Looks like Nordstrom dropped his oil pan. Dawkins spun out. So did Volmer and Harris. Settle down, Trey. It's going to be a while before they clean up this mess."

Seven more cars spun out and further expanded the oil slick. The next ten laps were driven under the caution flag. Fortunately Trey was out in front at the time.

The last five laps of the race were a three-way competition between Trey, Will Branch and Kent Grosso, each taking a lead lap. By the last one, Trey was in the number three position going into Turn One. He pulled up beside Branch on the short straightaway going into Turn Two and nosed ahead of him coming out of the ninety-degree angle. Grosso was a car length ahead of him on the backstretch. Trey took the dangerous inside of Turn Three, paralleled Grosso going into Turn Four and pulled ahead coming out of it. He zoomed across the finish line less than half a car length ahead of him.

Nicole hugged her brother. They danced up and down. The crowd in the grandstands exploded in cheers.

"Victory Lane, folks," Ethan exclaimed over the intercom. "Sweet."

Victory Lane was but the beginning of the formalities and festivities that followed winning a race. Interviews, handshakes and photo ops with officials and sponsors followed. As one onslaught waned another commenced. Hours slipped by before Trey was able to turn the microphone over to Gaby Colson, his PR rep, break loose and start back to his motor home for a shower and change of clothes, Nicole and Dave by his side. Normally, the enormous motor home would have pulled out soon after the race began, but because of the uncertainty of when Trey would return and the unexpected appearance of his visitor, he had asked his coach driver to stay over, regardless of the outcome of the race.

Outside the motor home, Dave stopped, drew himself up, crossed his arms and towered over both of them like a reproachful god.

"I've arranged to crash tonight with Adam—" who'd also elected to hang around "—so you two have the place completely to yourselves. I'd lock you in, if I knew how. It doesn't take a wise old man to see you've both been acting like a couple of dumb adolescents. So talk, work things out. Nobody's going to disturb you for the rest of the night."

Nicole looked up at her brother, torn between an impulse to laugh and another to cry. Her kid brother had taken on the role of big brother. It felt good, remarkably good. She shifted her attention to Trey. His face radiated a fierce pride. He winked at Dave, offered Nicole the crook of his arm. "I guess we'd better do as we're told."

CHAPTER TWENTY-THREE

ONCE INSIDE, HOWEVER, the mirth shimmering between them turned self-conscious and sober, and the lightheartedness morphed into a palpable tension. For a few moments they merely stared at each other, at a loss for words. It seemed to Trey they were both leaning forward, poised on the brink of a kiss, an embrace, yet neither of them was willing to make the first move. He could definitely forgive her for not wanting to get too close at the moment.

"I need to shower," he announced.

She nodded, then offered a thin smile. "Yes, you do."

He was hoping she might offer to scrub his back. He pictured the two of them, their bodies slick with soap, bubbles poised on curves and ridges, with nothing but warm water to cool the heat generated by each stroke of the washcloth.

When she showed no inclination to fulfill the fantasy, he resumed breathing and told her to make herself comfortable, reminded her needlessly that there was beer, wine and soft drinks as well as juice and bottled water in the refrigerator. He'd join her in a few minutes. "And there are snacks in the pantry," he added, reluctant to leave her.

She shrugged, refusing to meet his eyes. "I'm not hungry." She ambled to the couch, sat down, crossed one jeans-clad leg over the other and picked up a racing magazine from the coffee table.

He studied her for several seconds. The room was quiet but for the pounding in his ears. Emotions, erotic and affectionate, slithered through him. He loved this woman. He wanted her. He wanted her to want him. She glanced up, caught him watching and stopped her blind flipping of pages. "I thought you were going to shower."

She tried to sound impatient, but he detected tension in her voice. He continued to watch her in silence for a few more seconds, causing her to squirm. Smiling, he retreated to the bedroom but didn't completely close the door. He didn't want even the click of a latch separating them.

Fifteen minutes later, scrubbed and shaved, he emerged from the bedroom wearing khaki shorts and a light blue T-shirt, his feet bare. She was still sitting on the couch, the magazine spread open in her lap. He wondered if she'd read a word of it.

"I need a drink of water," he observed. "Then how about some wine? White or red? I have both."

"White, I guess." She put the magazine aside, climbed to her feet.

He dispensed chilled water from the door of the stainless-steel refrigerator, drank it down, then got out a bottle of pinot grigio, set two bulbous wineglasses on the black marble counter, poured moderate portions, recorked the bottle and returned it to the fridge.

She'd moved up to the counter, slipped one shapely hip onto the edge of a stool and observed his actions, but she was no more invested in the wine than he was. Her fingertips touched his as he slid the glass forward. The all-too-brief contact was like a zap of static electricity arcing between them. She raised her glass, drank too fast and fell into a fit of coughing.

He rushed around the end of the counter and, holding her one arm, thumped cautiously on her back. "You okay?"

"Went down the wrong pipe," she croaked. "I'll be all right in a minute."

He brought her a glass of water. She caught her breath enough to take a careful mouthful. He sat on the stool beside her, saying nothing. Waiting.

"Dave's grown up," she finally said, lifting the wineglass and allowing herself a conservative sip. "Thanks to you."

"He's been growing up for a long time."

"But I didn't see it." She rotated the stem of her glass. "Or maybe I didn't want to."

"It's hard to let go of kids, even irritating kid brothers, I imagine."

She huffed mildly. "How would you know?"

"I don't know, of course. I'm the youngest in the family, the one they always refer to as Little Brother." He made an attempt at a smile. "It's a heavy burden to carry."

She snorted, but as she raised her glass for another taste he caught the twinkle in her eye. "Dave isn't exactly little anymore."

"But he's still a teenager. He has a lot to learn, the second of which is that he has a lot to learn."

She raised an eyebrow in amusement. There was no mistaking the curiosity in her blue eyes. In a tone that said *okay, I'll bite,* she asked, "And the first?"

"How much he loves his sister for always being there for him."

She said nothing, didn't even nod her head, but he could see by the suppleness that came over her features that she appreciated his words.

"Let's take our drinks over there—" he swiveled on his stool and pointed to the living area "—where we can be more comfortable."

He let her take the lead and was disappointed when she

chose an upholstered chair instead of the couch. He accepted the latter and stretched his bare legs across the cool leather cushions.

"I realize now I've been too domineering, overprotective." She set her glass on the end table. "You've opened my eyes to a lot of things."

He wasn't sure it was a compliment. Were they still talking about her brother? "Dave loves you, don't ever doubt that. I hope you can also see I love you, too, though not like a brother. I want you in my life, Nicci, a part of my life, a part of me."

"I don't know why," she answered back. "You don't respect me enough to even inform me when you think you've had a seizure. If I hadn't shown up here when I did, would you have even bothered to tell me?"

He hung his head and marshaled the irritation that bubbled up. He wasn't going to let her put him on the defensive. "You don't know how many times I started to call you."

"But you didn't, Trey. That's the point. What could have been a life-changing event…" She let the words trail off, took a breath. "Did it occur to you that I might care what was happening to you, that I might want to be with you to share the crisis?"

He knew he'd wanted her there, but her response stunned him and seemed to justify his not calling her.

"Let me remind you," he retorted, "that you were the one who said we ought to cool it, who said we shouldn't see each other anymore. What was I supposed to think?"

She lowered her head, breaking what brief eye contact they'd managed since moving to the living room. But putting *her* on the defensive wouldn't bring them together, either. He sucked in a breath. He wanted to be imperturbable and rational, but frustration churned inside him. Frustration and desire and fear that he had lost her for good.

How could he get her to understand that his life was empty without her? He climbed to his feet, then knelt at hers. Under other circumstances he would have laughed at the startled expression on her face. But he wasn't laughing. He felt no joy, only worry, as he took her hands in his.

"My world has changed since I met you. What used to be enough isn't anymore. I feel incomplete without you. My happiness is dependent on your happiness. I measure my success now by the look in your eyes. I'm selfish, Nicci. I admit it. I want the best for me and the people I love, and the best thing for me is you. Without you everything else diminishes in value, becomes worthless."

She kept her eyes averted. He wasn't sure if it was out of embarrassment or annoyance. He released her hands and stood up.

"We have a lot in common, you and I. We're both focused, ambitious and independent." He began pacing in front of the blank wide-screen TV. "In your job you have to make quick decisions, sometimes with a minimum of information. The right decision may not achieve what you want or expect. The wrong one could be catastrophic, so you go on knowledge aided by instincts developed by years of training and observation. You don't always have the luxury of time to confer with colleagues, to study alternatives. You act and hope for the best."

He watched her and suspected she wasn't even aware she was nodding. He took encouragement that he'd finally made a connection.

"It's like NASCAR," he continued. "I have to make split-second decisions. I have to be able to count on other people for support, on mutual trust not only with my team but with my competitors. I don't have time to seek advice or to debate options, not at a hundred eighty miles per hour."

Her distant gaze told him he had her thinking. "I hadn't thought of it that way," she said.

"The need for each of us to make snap decisions," he went on, "has taught us bad habits."

Her head lifted. "What bad habits?" But there was more curiosity than offense in the challenge.

"You've made decisions for Dave without asking him what he wanted. That was understandable and necessary when he was younger, and I...I've made decisions that were well intended but that I had no right to make."

She stared directly at him.

"I'm sorry, Nicole," he said, "and I ask your forgiveness."

SHE WAS FEELING LIGHT-HEADED, and not because of two sips of wine. Trey Sanford was forever surprising her. Life would never be dull with this man.

He sat down again, arms flung out against the pillows in the corner of the couch. She jumped up, restless, uncertain, torn between her wants and her pride, between her needs and her longing. Stopping on the other side of the coffee table, she crossed her arms and looked down at him.

"Not forgiving you would be much easier, you know, if your decisions weren't always right." The hint of a self-satisfied smirk appeared in his blue eyes, but he was smart enough to squelch it. "And in this case," she continued, "your judgment happens to be right. I've come to realize, reluctantly, that I'm as controlling and overbearing as you are."

"Me? Overbearing?" He grinned up at her. It didn't

matter that she felt like a fool, she couldn't resist. She grinned back.

"I admit it," she said. "As much as I don't want to sometimes, I have to allow him to make his own decisions—"

"Even his own mistakes."

She sighed. "And hope in letting go he'll come back."

"He hasn't gone away."

"In my head I know you're right."

"But in your heart it's not so easy."

She returned to the easy chair and threw herself into it. "No, it isn't."

"I've let my heart overrule my brain these last few months," he acknowledged, then added in self-mockery, "and it's all your fault!"

She glared over at him. "My fault?"

"I made decisions because I wanted to please, to impress. I've been lucky. They turned out to be the right things to do, but the truth is I was doing them for the wrong reasons, and I ended up hurting you in the process."

He patted the seat beside him. She sat, her spine not quite touching the back of the couch. He placed his hand on her forearm. "Nicci, I nibble, but I don't bite." He gently coaxed her into the crook of his shoulder. With a chuckle, she rested against him, inhaled the scent of woodsy aftershave. Touching him felt so good.

"You said once that I've led a charmed life," he reminded her, his voice soft, intimate, so close to her ear. "You're right. Unfortunately all that wealth and indulgence, well intended though it might have been, also robbed me of an important lesson in life, a lesson you've taught me, that sometimes you have to give up selfish desires for the good of others. You gave up your athletic ambitions and delayed medical school so your brother could have the home he needed and deserved."

"I'm no saint," she objected, and placed her hand on his chest. Beneath the ridge of hard pectoral muscle, his heart beat. "I did what I had to do, like most people in this world."

"Well, now it's my turn to do something for other people."

She turned her head and looked up at him. "What are you talking about?"

"You were right that nothing destroys a stereotype better than an exception to the rule. I've been an exception my entire life. The son of a famous—and notorious—NASCAR driver. The brother of another NASCAR driver who was forced out in disgrace. And being a NASCAR driver myself. That charmed life you spoke of. Then there's the other exception. I have a seizure disorder, epilepsy, yet I can still drive in NASCAR."

"What you said is true, but—"

"I've decided to go public with my epilepsy," he announced. "Maybe it'll help other people with seizure disorders be better understood, less discriminated against, more comfortable in their own skin."

She sat forward, pulling out of his gentle embrace, and twisted around to face him. "Trey, you can't."

"I know it'll cause a few problems. I'll have to trust my fellow drivers, my fans and sponsors to recognize that my success has been *in spite of* my disorder, that I'm no more a danger to anyone today than I was yesterday."

"There you go again—" she shot to her feet and glared down at him "—making a decision without talking to anyone about it."

"But—"

"Look, Trey, I appreciate what you want to do and why, but it would be a mistake, a big, big mistake."

"But you were the one who wanted me to—"

"I should never have brought up the idea to begin with. You were absolutely right to call me crazy for even suggesting it." She shook her head. "Go back to using your head instead of your heart. You would be giving up a multimillion-dollar career, a life you love, and you would gain nothing for it. You've had a very good reason for keeping your disorder secret. You would sow the seeds of doubt and distrust not only among your fellow drivers but among the public, and you'd probably lose sponsors in the process."

She again subsided against him, this time taking his hands in hers and pressing them to her cheek. "Oh, honey, your heart is on the right track, but don't go public. Not now. Not yet. Wait until you retire, when people can no longer hurt you professionally, when you have a long record of accomplishments to point back to as proof you were not affected by the disorder. That'll be the time for you to go public. In the meantime, it would be better for you to become an advocate for the cause without appearing to have a vested interest in it."

"You're something else." He kissed the top of her head, brought her body in tighter contact with his. Desire rolled through her like a tidal wave. "I thought you'd be pleased."

"I am pleased that you want to do this—" she smiled "—pleased and touched. It's one of the things I love about you, that you think of others, that you're willing to act on their behalf. You didn't have to make yourself vulnerable by telling Dave about your epilepsy. You didn't have to arrange for him to get a VNS or buy him a new car. You didn't have to spend your precious few free hours coming to the clinic and volunteering your time. There was nothing in it for you, doing those things."

He grinned. "I got to see you."

She laughed and shook her head. "You could have done

that without doing those things, and you know it. You call yourself selfish. I disagree. I think you're one of the most generous people I've ever met."

She couldn't help smiling at his embarrassment. Humble Trey. The strange and wonderful thing was that, for all the hype and bravado, he was humble. He took his joy in the act of giving, in the happiness of the recipient, not in the praise and adulation that might result. If he had wanted recognition, he wouldn't have come to the clinic as Carter Brooks.

As if he had been reading her mind and was eager to contradict her, he said, "You do wonders for my ego."

She arched her brows. "I hope my influence isn't limited to your psyche."

He laughed, and she could feel his body vibrate against hers at the same time the anxiety that had been a part of her for so long began to dissipate.

She grinned from ear to ear. "No, I guess it isn't."

"A very astute observation."

"I'm a very astute person."

"I was going to say sexy."

"Oh, okay, say sexy."

He laughed and swallowed her in his arms. "Hmm, sexy. Yes, very sexy. Speaking of which, shall we adjourn to the bedroom?"

"What's wrong with the couch?"

"Um…"

She laughed. "If you prefer the bedroom, that's fine. I know you're used to your creature comforts."

"Actually there is something I want to talk to you about."

"I guess that means we're not going to the bedroom."

"We can talk about it in there."

"Do you think we will?"

"Hmm. Good point." He toyed with the top button of her blouse.

She closed her eyes, enjoying the tingling sensation his manipulations prompted. "So what did you want to talk about?"

"You're getting very aggressive." He ran the side of his finger down her temple and cheek.

"I like to be on top of things," she pointed out.

HE THROBBED WITH LAUGHTER. "Oh, baby," he murmured, then wrapped his arms around her and kissed her with a passion whetted by pent-up desire, fear of losing her—he would never take her for granted again—and a need that went beyond the moment.

"Now what did you want to talk about?" she taunted.

"Uh…"

She stretched herself luxuriously against him, snickering at his reaction. "Cat got your tongue?" She kissed his forehead.

"I…uh…"

She kissed his eyelids.

"Don't…have…"

She kissed the tip of his nose.

"A…cat."

She grinned at him. "Maybe we'll get one," she said softly, then kissed his mouth. For the next minutes they were lost in each other's senses.

"That's—" he fought to get control of himself "—what I wanted to talk to you about."

She rolled to the side of him, releasing some of the pressure, but far from all. He was looking forward to their exorcising more of it, but he knew his desire for her would never go away. She looked at him. "A cat?"

He took in the sight of her features, inhaled her scent,

gloried in the warmth of her body against his. "Us. Now that we've agreed we're so much alike, I'm hoping you'll lift the edict that we not see each other anymore."

She giggled. "I think that's already been established."

"So now that we're seeing each other again and acknowledge that we love each other… You do love me, don't you?"

She shook her head, clearly amused by his fumbling with words. "I think that's been established, too."

"Good. Good."

She kissed him gently but pulled away when he started to deepen it. "Why don't you get it out, say what you want to say?"

"I'm trying to, but you—" He laughed and glided his hand up her neck to her ear, tangled his fingers in her hair and guided her mouth down to his. He took his time. "I don't ever want to lose you, Nicci. I'll do anything to make you happy. Will…will you marry me?"

IT WAS PATHETIC, she thought to herself, that she wanted to cry. She wasn't sure why. Out of happiness? Out of fear? Because she couldn't say yes.

Wasn't this where a relationship with a man was supposed to lead? At least for her. And not any man, the man who dominated her thoughts and had taken possession of her heart. So why was she surprised at his proposal? Why didn't she simply give in to her impulse and say yes? She'd already admitted she loved him, and she believed him when he said he loved her. So why was she hesitating?

"I know we have some lifestyle issues to work out," he said. It was uncanny the way he anticipated her, the way he was able to read her mind. "I would never ask you to give up your profession. Or the house. We share a love of books.

We share so much, Nicci. I want you, I need you to be a part of my life, and I want to be a part of yours. I love you."

This time she did cry.

"Honey?" The concern in his voice brought laughter through the tears, the laughter of happiness, of joy.

She bracketed his face, squeezed his cheeks so that they puckered his mouth, then she kissed his lips. "I love you, Trey, and I want to marry you. But I'm a control freak, remember? Can I think about it?"

"For as long as it takes."

She remembered the exhilarating feeling she'd gotten at the airport when she'd been impulsive and signed up for standby here to Indianapolis.

"Oh, shoot," she exclaimed, "I know what the answer will be. Yes, Trey, I'll marry you."

* * * * *

Celebrate 60 years of pure reading pleasure with Harlequin®!

To commemorate the event, Silhouette Special Edition invites you to Ashley O'Ballivan's bed-and-breakfast in the small town of Stone Creek. The beautiful innkeeper will have her hands full caring for her old flame Jack McCall. He's on the run and recovering from a mysterious illness, but that won't stop him from trying to win Ashley back.

Enjoy an exclusive glimpse of Linda Lael Miller's
AT HOME IN STONE CREEK.
Available in November 2009 from
Silhouette Special Edition®.

The helicopter swung abruptly sideways in a dizzying arch, setting Jack McCall's fever-ravaged brain spinning.

His friend's voice sounded tinny, coming through the earphones. "You belong in a hospital," he said. "Not some backwater bed-and-breakfast."

All Jack really knew about the virus raging through his system was that it wasn't contagious, and there was no known treatment for it besides a lot of rest and quiet. "I don't like hospitals," he responded, hoping he sounded like his normal self. "They're full of sick people."

Vince Griffin chuckled but it was a dry sound, rough at the edges. "What's in Stone Creek, Arizona?" he asked. "Besides a whole lot of nothin'?"

Ashley O'Ballivan was in Stone Creek, and she was a whole lot of somethin', but Jack had neither the strength nor the inclination to explain. After the way he'd ducked out six months before, he didn't expect a welcome, knew he didn't deserve one. But Ashley, being Ashley, would take him in whatever her misgivings.

He had to get to Ashley; he'd be all right.

He closed his eyes, letting the fever swallow him.

There was no telling how much time had passed when he became aware of the chopper blades slowing overhead. Dimly, he saw the private ambulance waiting on the airfield outside of Stone Creek; it seemed that twilight had descended.

Jack sighed with relief. His clothes felt clammy against his flesh. His teeth began to chatter as two figures unloaded a gurney from the back of the ambulance and waited for the blades to stop.

"Great," Vince remarked, unsnapping his seat belt. "Those two look like volunteers, not real EMTs."

The chopper bounced sickeningly on its runners, and Vince, with a shake of his head, pushed open his door and jumped to the ground, head down.

Jack waited, wondering if he'd be able to stand on his own. After fumbling unsuccessfully with the buckle on his seat belt, he decided not.

When it was safe the EMTs approached, following Vince, who opened Jack's door.

His old friend Tanner Quinn stepped around Vince, his grin not quite reaching his eyes.

"You look like hell warmed over," he told Jack cheerfully.

"Since when are you an EMT?" Jack retorted.

Tanner reached in, wedged a shoulder under Jack's right arm and hauled him out of the chopper. His knees immediately buckled, and Vince stepped up, supporting him on the other side.

"In a place like Stone Creek," Tanner replied, "everybody helps out."

They reached the wheeled gurney, and Jack found himself on his back.

Tanner and the second man strapped him down, a process that brought back a few bad memories.

"Is there even a hospital in this place?" Vince asked irritably from somewhere in the night.

"There's a pretty good clinic over in Indian Rock,"

Tanner answered easily, "and it isn't far to Flagstaff." He paused to help his buddy hoist Jack and the gurney into the back of the ambulance. "You're in good hands, Jack. My wife is the best veterinarian in the state."

Jack laughed raggedly at that.

Vince muttered a curse.

Tanner climbed into the back beside him, perched on some kind of fold-down seat. The other man shut the doors.

"You in any pain?" Tanner said as his partner climbed into the driver's seat and started the engine.

"No." Jack looked up at his oldest and closest friend and wished he'd listened to Vince. Ever since he'd come down with the virus—a week after snatching a five-year-old girl back from her non-custodial parent, a small-time Colombian drug dealer—he hadn't been able to think about anyone or anything but Ashley. When he *could* think, anyway.

Now, in one of the first clearheaded moments he'd experienced since checking himself out of Bethesda the day before, he realized he might be making a major mistake. Not by facing Ashley—he owed her that much and a lot more. No, he could be putting her in danger, putting Tanner and his daughter and his pregnant wife in danger, too.

"I shouldn't have come here," he said, keeping his voice low.

Tanner shook his head, his jaw clamped down hard as though he was irritated by Jack's statement.

"This is where you belong," Tanner insisted. "If you'd had sense enough to know that six months ago, old buddy, when you bailed on Ashley without so much as a fare-thee-well, you wouldn't be in this mess."

Ashley. The name had run through his mind a million times in those six months, but hearing somebody say it out loud was like having a fist close around his insides and squeeze hard.

Jack couldn't speak.

Tanner didn't press for further conversation.

The ambulance bumped over country roads, finally hitting smooth blacktop.

"Here we are," Tanner said. "Ashley's place."

* * * * *

Will Jack be able to patch things up with Ashley,
or will his past put the woman he loves in harm's way?
Find out in
AT HOME IN STONE CREEK
by Linda Lael Miller.
Available November 2009 from
Silhouette Special Edition®.

REQUEST YOUR FREE BOOKS!

2 FREE NOVELS PLUS 2 FREE GIFTS!

Silhouette®

SPECIAL EDITION®

Life, Love and Family!

YES! Please send me 2 FREE Silhouette Special Edition® novels and my 2 FREE gifts (gifts are worth about $10). After receiving them, if I don't wish to receive any more books, I can return the shipping statement marked "cancel." If I don't cancel, I will receive 6 brand-new novels every month and be billed just $4.24 per book in the U.S. or $4.99 per book in Canada. That's a savings of at least 15% off the cover price! It's quite a bargain! Shipping and handling is just 50¢ per book.* I understand that accepting the 2 free books and gifts places me under no obligation to buy anything. I can always return a shipment and cancel at any time. Even if I never buy another book from Silhouette, the two free books and gifts are mine to keep forever.

235 SDN EYN4   335 SDN EYPG

Name _____ (PLEASE PRINT) _____

Address _____ Apt. # _____

City _____ State/Prov. _____ Zip/Postal Code _____

Signature (if under 18, a parent or guardian must sign) _____

Mail to the **Silhouette Reader Service:**
IN U.S.A.: P.O. Box 1867, Buffalo, NY 14240-1867
IN CANADA: P.O. Box 609, Fort Erie, Ontario L2A 5X3

Not valid to current subscribers of Silhouette Special Edition books.

Want to try two free books from another line?
Call 1-800-873-8635 or visit www.morefreebooks.com.

* Terms and prices subject to change without notice. Prices do not include applicable taxes. Sales tax applicable in N.Y. Canadian residents will be charged applicable provincial taxes and GST. Offer not valid in Quebec. This offer is limited to one order per household. All orders subject to approval. Credit or debit balances in a customer's account(s) may be offset by any other outstanding balance owed by or to the customer. Please allow 4 to 6 weeks for delivery. Offer available while quantities last.

Your Privacy: Silhouette is committed to protecting your privacy. Our Privacy Policy is available online at www.eHarlequin.com or upon request from the Reader Service. From time to time we make our lists of customers available to reputable third parties who may have a product or service of interest to you. If you would prefer we not share your name and address, please check here. ☐

SSE09R